Without Rolo, there would be no Secret Adventures.
He snuck into my life when the children were all but
grown up offering unconditional love, and became
my fourth child. Like them, he brings daily laughter,
joy and structure to my midlife and he is the reason
I have opened my eyes to the beauty of nature on a
daily basis.

This book is dedicated to rescue dogs and their
owners everywhere. And to the friends who
empowered and encouraged me to write down his
story, the bits he couldn't write himself.

Notes on Marlborough

Marlborough is a thriving market town in north east Wiltshire not far from junction 15 of the M4.

Prehistoric remains prove early settlement, and the town once boasted a fine castle and royal mint. Two old churches and the fine 17th century Merchant House nestle in the famously wide High Street which runs along the old coaching route between London and Bristol and Bath (now the A4).

The River Kennet meanders through the town. Marlborough is edged by Savernake Forest, former hunting ground of kings, and above the town you will find a fine common. Other nearby places of interest includes Hungerford, Devizes, Silbury Hill, Avebury, Fyfield and Pewsey.

Contents

www.debievans.com

Prologue

Emerging from the time tunnel and waving off the tiny lamp bearers, I nearly bolted back down the hole after them. There were lots of loud bangs and fireworks lighting up the sky. Only they weren't fireworks – not the brightly coloured ones the floppy haired boy lights to celebrate Guy Fawkes Night at the beginning of November anyway. (I'm not scared of fireworks by the way, just angry about them. How dare people let them off in my garden?)

No – these were seriously loud bangs and I WAS scared. Suddenly the noise stopped and I could smell smoke. I ran about yapping as I don't like fire. There were sirens going off and that nearly sent me crazy – I don't even like it when the floppy haired boy leaves the fridge open and it beeps. Then a man in a white tin helmet that said ARP on it caught me by the collar and said,

"Are you a rescue dog? Come quickly. We need you over here."

7

I could see there was a commotion. Something terrible had happened. I followed where he pointed. We found ourselves standing next to the remains of a building which had just become a mass of rubble.

Chapter 1

Rolo Comes Home

The door of the old barn in which we were contained creaked open. It wasn't meal time. I glanced up and saw a smiley lady and a boy with floppy hair. The other homeless dogs went crazy, same old routine of barking and jumping up every time someone came in, "pick me, pick me!" Silly fools. Don't they realise the louder they bark, the more they put off prospective owners? I've been around the block a few times. Believe me I know.

I stayed very still and quiet in the corner of my pen, gathering my feet together in a little bundle and looking down. This was a very different tactic. The smiley lady seemed close to tears and the boy was flitting around from pen to pen and the dogs growing more and more excited at the thought of finding a new home with these kindly looking strangers. We were all shapes and sizes, ages and colours but the thing that united us was that we were all pre-loved and pretty desperate.

At this point I should introduce myself; I am a tricoloured Jack Russell, currently called Ronnie, but I don't answer to that. The smiley lady took one look at my toffee and chocolate coloured face and said I should be called Rolo. Smiley lady, you can call me anything you like as long as you take me home and love me forever. I kept my thoughts to myself and my dark brown eyes discreetly to the ground.
She hadn't moved on. I could sense without looking up that she was still standing in front of me. I just had to time the next bit right and I'd be going home

10

with her.

'Rolo' she said softly. I liked the way she said it. I looked up shyly the way I had been practising: big brown pools of melting chocolate eyes. How could she resist? She called the boy with floppy hair over.

"This one" she said quietly.

"Are you sure Mum? He doesn't seem very keen," said the boy with floppy hair.

Little did he know this was my well-rehearsed act to reel them in.

One of the staff brought my lead and the floppy haired boy took me into a big field right next to the Rescue Centre. We walked for a while and I kept glancing back at them over my shoulder to make sure they were still there. The smiley lady kept taking photographs and saying how cute I was. The boy was not convinced. I had my work cut out with him. Time to up my game. When they sat down on a bench I jumped up on the boy's lap and licked him under his chin. He laughed. That was it; I had 'em.

Two more visits, and I tried not to look too keen, afraid of rejection again, and then the paperwork was completed. Their garden was visited by someone from the Rescue place to make sure it was terrier proof (we are famed for our tunnelling skills) and the smiley lady was advised to have me for a sleepover before she signed on the dotted line, as it was on record that I had been returned several times. At this point they told her I didn't like other dogs, rain or long walks.

The smiley lady made a noise something like a snort, grabbed the pen, signed her name with a flourish and handed over a donation. I heard her say that she would feel that she had failed the dog not that the dog had failed her if things didn't work out. I loved her from that moment. And so I went to my fourth new home.

The smiley lady talked and sang to me all the way

The Secret Adventures of Rolo

home. She lifted me into a sort of pop up tent which was wedged on the back seat of the car and zipped it up. I could still see out though…the walls had mesh windows. She could see me in the driving mirror. The floppy haired boy and his friends were waiting at home after school, peering out from the lounge window, anxious to greet the new playmate. I knew what was expected of me: played a bit, ran around, jumped on their laps, licked them and they squealed with delight when I did my 'meerkat' routine, standing up on my back legs when they offered me a doggy biscuit.

When the other boys had gone home it was just me and the smiley lady and the floppy haired boy. They showed me my bed and I jumped straight in. And it was a brand new basket, big enough for an Alsatian. I'd never had one of those before. It had a pillow and blankets and everything. This home would be different – I just knew it. The garden was fun to explore…I swear I could smell cats and even more excitingly, next door they had rabbits – proper outdoor ones, and I could smell them through the

13

wooden fence. I could push my nose through a knot hole in one of the upright planks and really savour the aroma of live rabbit! At the bottom of the garden there was a gate. I longed to explore whatever might be beyond, but that would have to wait until another day. I had no idea at this point that beyond the gate lay untold mysteries and that going through the gate was when the adventure would really begin.

When it was really night time outside, the smiley lady and the floppy haired boy called me in from the garden and shut me in the darkened kitchen, tucking me into my new bed telling me to be a good boy. Wait a minute! Didn't they tell them at the dogs' home that I have a separation anxiety and don't like being left alone? I'd much rather curl up with the floppy haired boy on his bed. So I whined… and then I howled.

After a while, footsteps approached. The lady came to the door but she didn't open it. 'Bed' she said firmly in a tone that meant she was serious. It wasn't so bad here and I didn't want to appear ungrateful, so I decided to give in and, exhausted from all the crying, I eventually dropped off to sleep.

A few days later, whilst the floppy haired boy was at school, I taught myself how to use his lap top and started writing a blog. The thing is he's always talking outloud when he is doing schoolwork on his laptop, explaining different functions of keys and software (I think it helps him remember) and I'm taking it all in. I even know his password. The floppy haired boy is always making jokes about what I would be able to do if only I had thumbs that could work like human thumbs can (I can't remember what he called it) – how amazed he would be if he knew I could type!

15

Dog blog #1 According to Rolo

Well, what an exhausting and exciting life I'm leading. I say 'lead' because I'm still on one. Way too excited to listen to many commands just yet but boy have I covered some Wiltshire miles and done some serious exploring. I had never encountered long grass in my previous homes,and today I almost caught a squirrel! If it wasn't for the bloomin' lead I would have been up the tree after it! I did get told off though for another reason. I'd been having way too much fun romping through the undergrowth in the smiley lady's garden and found something new to play with. A fledgling blackbird. Only it didn't want to play and seemed to go to sleep. Its angry parents were still shrieking at me when I went back

out into the garden later today,the
smiley lady stopped smiling and
said she was 'disappointed', but
she understands that I am a hunter
and I think I am forgiven.

There is something under the
decking in the back garden which
needs more exploring. I think it's
a mouse. I can smell it but I can't
see it. I keep going out there to
check it out. I put my eyeball to
the slats in the decking and sniff
and sniff but the secret garden
resident hasn't revealed itself to
me yet. I will find it. All for now;
more later. I don't want my people
to know I can blog.

A bedtime routine in the house was being
established but I still didn't like being shut in at
night. My people would put me out in the garden
last thing before they went upstairs and first thing in

the morning, whatever the weather, and being smart I quickly realised, by way of a rewards system, that I wasn't supposed to wee in the kitchen. I knew it was my cue to go outside when they said the magic word 'cats' and the door would suddenly fly open. I couldn't get out there quick enough. Cats? Not on MY territory! Oh well, might as well have a wee whilst I'm out here... We are getting to understand each other, the people and I.

After three days in my wonderful new home, the lady took me down the garden steps and out through a rickety old gate into a huge woodland full of interesting smells and the promise of something exciting - could it be adventure? - hung in the air.

She made me sit and gave me a stern lecture about not running out of earshot and then she let me off the lead for the very first time. There were a few other dogs to meet and greet with a wag and a sniff. Some I'm sure I recognised from the Rescue place... they were all behaving themselves too; we were all keen to impress our new owners, just in case they treated us like library books, kept for a while and then returned. But my smiley lady had promised she wouldn't do that. I was for keeps.

We dogs had a secret code, a message we passed on to each other, 'keep calm, fit in, you'll be fine.' This was whispered to the front end and the back end, from dog to dog. I loved this wood it was so big and exciting. It was the bestest place I'd ever been to! Surely it must be magical!

As soon as the gate creaked open and I was let off the lead, the anticipation of wildlife to chase and marvellous scents to follow almost overwhelmed me - I couldn't help but let out a little whimper of excitement - bracken, deer, foxes, birds all ever so exciting, but still I had this huge fear of being shut in the kitchen and away from my people at night. Every night I whined and every night I howled and every night the lady told me firmly through the closed door: 'BED'.

Chapter 2

The Adventure Begins

Just a few days into my idyllic new life, something happened that completely changed my little rescued doggy world and cured my fear of bedtime isolation once and for all - it happened like this:

It was May and the woods were carpeted with blue flowers that shook and tinkled in the breeze releasing a heady scent. I was off the lead and running free and as usual I kept glancing behind… the smiley lady and the floppy haired boy were chatting about his upcoming exams at school and how he should be preparing for them.

I went off on an adventure, following the scent of something earthy and exciting and I soon forgot to keep them within earshot. On and on I charged, flattening the bell flowers with my paws…off the footpath, under a bush and into a clearing and then I heard a little voice…it wasn't the lady or the boy…

it was very gruff and obviously belonged to someone quite small,

 "Oi, Paddy Paws, mind what you're doing!"

I snuffled in the undergrowth, getting my nose very wet indeed from the early morning dew and was just about to raise my leg against a very old oak tree when I came face to face with a tiny angry person, who looked like a little doll. To my surprise the weeny man smacked me on the nose. He bent down to pick up something and was waving this prickly thing at me that quite resembled a baby hedgehog. It was in fact the casing of a Sweet Chestnut presumably left over from a squirrel's larder last autumn. It was sharp. I backed away, put my head on one side and watched the man quizzically, just out of range of the offending prickles.

"Now you listen here, Paddy Paws, this is a very special tree and it doesn't need any mutts watering it thank you very much."

I sat down on my haunches and gathered my feet together, keeping my eyes firmly on the tiny angry man. He clambered over a very large tree root and beckoned for someone else to come and see. Out from the green mossy foliage stepped a tiny woman with long black hair wearing a dress; he blended in so well to the velvety green covering on the tree root she could barely be seen.

"Yulia, look, here's another one of them pesky paddy paws - I stopped him just as he was about to water the ancient gateway!"

The little lady doll called Yulia tiptoed towards me and I bent my face down so she could reach and she tickled my ear and then moved round and tenderly stroked my nose.

"There, there, Paddy Paws…now then, Da, it's not his fault; he doesn't know. Trees are magnets to dogs…they really can't help themselves."

"The name's Rolo," I said and both small folk jumped

up in the air in fright and ducked down behind the nearest tree root.

"He talks!" the one called Da whispered in amazement, peering cautiously over the top of the parapet.

"I'm sorry if I startled you," I said "and apologies, I didn't mean any harm to your gateway. Where does it lead to? What is on the other side…more woods to play in?"

"Sorry Paddy Paws…we can't tell you. Only those that have the gift can enter the Understory. Athelstan will tell you."

I was dying to know who Athelstan was. Another dog perhaps? And what on earth was the Understory?

Suddenly I could hear my people calling in the distance, their voices followed by a sharp whistle… the floppy haired boy had been practicing! The small

23

folk disappeared down among the tree roots.

"Don't step on the trees toes," Yulia's muffled voice called from the undergrowth. I turned in the direction of the voices. As I glanced back over my shoulder I could see the outline of a strange creature wrapped around the tree trunk, blending into the bark. I swear it winked at me. I must be going mad! Trees can't wink!

24

"If you are meant to go through the gateway little pup you will know…" the barky voice said.

"What do you mean?" I spun round, frantic with curiosity. Wait a minute…trees can't talk either! I could hear human voices louder now…my people were coming nearer. All my instincts told me that, much as I loved them, I didn't want them to find this talking tree.

"You will know if you are chosen," Athelstan repeated as he faded into the tree bark.

I scrambled back out through the undergrowth and down the footpath, remembering the way I had come, and jumped into the arms of the floppy haired boy to distract him. I really didn't want him to find the Athelstan tree.

"Thank goodness Rolo…naughty boy…where have you been?" the smiley lady seemed very anxious as she caught up, slightly out of breath, and as I couldn't tell her how sorry I was for alarming her,

I wanted to make amends so I jumped down from the boy's arms and leapt up at her and nipped at her fingers. That was our secret sign. She would know I was sorry. She brushed my muddy footprints from her jeans and ruffled my ears. I was back in favour

and the mysterious talking tree was still my secret. On the way out from the woods, something caught the eye of the boy with the floppy hair and he bent down and retrieved a pink spiky ball among the leaves. It must have been dropped and rolled into the bluebells, lying quite undiscovered in the green leaves for goodness knows how long.

He threw it as far as he could and of course I chased

it and brought it back to him. I wouldn't drop it though. It was small and rubbery in texture and fitted exactly into my mouth. It had a little hole in it and was very pliable. I liked the feel of it and I could puff little breaths of air through it.

"Look, he loves it!" shouted the boy. "Drop, Rolo, drop!"

I wouldn't put the ball down and trotted all the way home; back through the gate and up the steps, through the garden and stood patiently on the recycling box whilst I had my paws wiped and I was firmly brushed; all the while clutching the precious pink ball in my mouth.

We had lots of games that evening. The floppy haired boy would take the pink ball off me and hide it and then I would find it and take it back to him and so it would go on. Then we played my favourite game of HTB (hide the biscuit). The lady and the boy would shut me out of the lounge whilst they hid a doggy treat. What they didn't realise is that there were glass panels in the door and I could see exactly where they were hiding it. 'Clever boy,' they said. I didn't let on. The biscuit was my reward.

That night I was tucked up in bed as usual and I dropped the pink ball into my basket so I would know where to find it when I wanted it. The kitchen door was shut firmly and I was told to 'sleep tight'. I only whined a bit. I was gradually becoming secure in the knowledge that they would come and open the door the next day.

Chapter 3

Rolo Meets Athelstan

Da, I discovered, although no more than two inches tall, is a wise old country man of goodness knows how many years, and he is always spouting folk lore wisdom. Much of what he knows I fear might be lost on the children of today. Certainly the floppy haired boy doesn't seem to know the names of the birds in the garden nor the trees in the forest.

Da on the other hand seems to know exactly what is happening in nature during any given month of the year; trees, flowers, birds, butterflies, animals, they all follow a set pattern dependant on the weather, and I thought I would share this with you as I learn from the woodland folk in case you don't know it either.

Then all you need to do is to take the time to stand still outdoors, away from the town or village you live in and open your eyes wide and look and listen to

29

the wonder of nature all around you.

Da's folklore wisdom for May: "Water in May brings bread through all the year."

The time when triangular candle shapes of white flowers grace the horse chestnut trees, promising a good crop of conkers in the autumn.

Bluebells carpet the woods. Bees and butterflies emerge over clover-filled fields and cow parsley can first be seen lacing the hedgerows. Buttercups, daisies, dandelions, birds foot trefoil, celandine, these are all keen to grace our downs and meadows.

Apple trees are in full blossom, hinting at delicious autumn fruit harvests to come. If you are very lucky you might hear a late cuckoo. Once heard never forgotten. Swifts and swallows arrive with the

promise of summer on their wing. In the
tall elm trees young rooks test their flying
equipment; stretching black wings. You might
hear a peewit call over pastures, named
for the sound it makes.

Blackbird, wren, robin, chaffinch and all
manner of birds join the garden choir in fine
voice. Meadow browns, chalk hill blues, small
coppers, early butterflies and many moths
are seeking the new meadow flowers. Field
mice, fox cubs, moles, stoats, water voles,
rabbits, hedgehogs and weasels can all be
seen by those who go quietly and have keen
eyesight.

The Secret Adventures of Rolo

The next morning, as hoped for, the sun peeked around the blackout curtain and I was surprised that the boy let me out for my early morning constitutional; it was usually the smiley lady. After breakfast he announced that he would take me for my woodland walk.

I could hardly wait and was so excited when I saw him fetch my lead from the hook by the front door. I wouldn't sit still to allow him to fasten it and when he sat down on the stairs to put his trainers on I kept jumping on his lap. He buried his face in my fur and I could hear him laughing. This was a great game.

He led me down the steps and through the rickety gate. I was pulling and jumping in my excitement!

I couldn't wait to be off the lead and as soon as I was unclipped, away I ran. I had the pink ball in my mouth. I glanced back at him over my shoulder a few times but he already had his mobile phone out and seemed too preoccupied to be watching me. I seized my chance and dived off under the

bushes into the familiar clearing. As I approached
the gnarled oak tree I saw Athelstan take shape and
realised that he was something quite separate from
the tree and seemed to be able to appear at will. The
old gatekeeper greeted me with a word I'd not heard
before that sounded something like 'wes hael'.

'That's not my name – I'm Rolo' but I kept my
thoughts to myself as I didn't wish to appear
impolite to this venerable creature. I don't know
what sort of mythical creature he was; he looked a
little bit like a friendly dragon.

I bowed my head to the tree guardian as his manner
seemed to command some kind of respect, and as I
did so I accidentally dropped the pink ball from my
mouth. It rolled between the tree roots and to my
dismay, fell into a hole. I didn't like that at all and
immediately went after it, sticking my head down
into the dark abyss under the tree.

'That's the way little pup, I thought you were chosen,'
said Athelstan from his camouflage of bark.

33

To my surprise the hole at the foot of the tree widened out and I could see the pink ball nestled on a root, just below the woodland floor. I poked my nose in just far enough to reach it, realising that I could actually go down that hole if I wanted to – it seemed to be a kind of passageway and we Jack Russells love tunnelling!

"ROLO!" and then a loud whistle. I heard the floppy haired boy in the distance – he must have just noticed that I'd gone missing. I snatched up the pink ball and wriggled backwards from the hole, tail first.

No time to explore it now. I had to get back to the wood side of the clearing to keep it secret.

Reunited with the floppy haired boy we heard an almighty commotion coming from the topmost branches of a nearby ash tree. The floppy haired boy was pointing and counting the squawking black and white birds. 'Morning my lord, morning my lord, morning my lord' he repeated over and over again, greeting each in turn.

"Well I've never seen seven magpies before, Rolo – I can't remember what seven are for." He repeated the traditional rhyme out loud:

"One for sorrow
Two for joy
Three for a girl
And four for a boy
Five for silver
Six for gold
Seven for a secret ready to be told."

I wondered if this could possibly be something to do with my recent secret discovery in the forest. I kept my wonderings to myself of course. We went home and I was rewarded with a biscuit for coming back when the floppy haired boy called me. Actually I'd rather have one of his chocolate biscuits.

The Secret Adventures of Rolo

Chapter 4

Understory Adventure – Rolo in the Medieval Forest

That night, tucked into my bed without so much as a whimper, and hearing the kitchen door firmly shut, I heard a tapping on the window behind the blackout curtain. My first instinct was to bark and wake the house up, but my curiosity got the better of me. I jumped up onto the counter with the aid of a stool and ran along the length of the work top, tiptoed over the cooker and passed the kettle, carefully stepping over used mugs, a dirty teaspoon and a jar of coffee, until I reached the sink.

I stuck my nose behind the window blind and nudged at it until my face was behind. It was very dark but I could just make out the shape of a large bird, possibly an owl, perched on the window ledge, tapping away and clearly trying to get my attention.

"Can I help you?" I enquired politely.

A tiny voice came from behind the birds head, muffled by the feathers,

"Athelstan sent us, Paddy Paws. He wants you to come and says to tell you that you must bring the orb." I recognised the voice as belonging to Yulia last seen clambering down among the tree roots in the forest, but now seated on the owl's back, easily recognisable by her mossy coloured green dress in the moonlight.

"But how do I get out of the house? I'm shut in the kitchen and I'm not allowed out on my own after dark!" I remonstrated.

"If you are the pup Athelstan thinks you are, you will work it out" said Yulia as she gripped the owl's neck feathers tightly and dug in with her heels and knees and at that, the night bird gathered itself up to a great height and flew off across the garden, over the tree tops, swallowed up by the inky black sky.

What on earth do I do now? I didn't know what was expected of me so I jumped down onto the tiled floor and went back to my basket. I curled up trying to sleep but something was digging into me. Investigation showed I was lying on the pink ball and it was rather uncomfortable so I wriggled round and picked it up in my mouth. It started to glow.

Holy Moly! I dropped it on the floor and it stopped glowing. I picked it up in my mouth and it glowed

again. This was a new game! I carried it over to the
cupboard under the sink. The door was left slightly
open as if someone hadn't put the floor cleaning
fluid away properly. Probably the smiley lady – I
can't imagine it would have been the boy with the
floppy hair. He only came into the kitchen to open
the fridge and stare at its contents. I curled my paw
around the crack and pulled the cupboard door
open and poked my nose in.

To my surprise, with the dusters, cloths, bottles
and bucket parted I could clearly make out a small
dog-sized trapdoor under the sink behind the
u-bend and surely heading to the great outside! I
put the pink ball down carefully on the floor of the
cupboard and nudged my way in.

The Secret Adventures of Rolo

I caught hold of the metal ring on the trapdoor with my teeth and pulled with all my might. Oops, I think I may have loosened a tooth! No time to worry about that now. The trapdoor opened easily enough, knocking over the cleaning paraphernalia under the kitchen sink and I thought I could smell the Great Outside…an exciting and earthy aroma, special night time scents.

My nose was twitching and I was suddenly on full hunting alert. As an afterthought I picked up the pink ball as a sort of comfort blanket and without too much worry as to where it all might lead, I squeezed myself through the trapdoor and there I was alone and outside in the scary but exciting dark of night!

Down the steps, past the flower beds, without so much as a glance at the mysterious inhabitant under the decking, under the rickety gate and on, on into the dark wood. I ran all the way. This was a big adventure for me as I am not usually allowed out on my own, let alone at night! I had to be brave; I had my pink ball in my mouth and I rushed ahead, following my nose until I found the right bushes. Squashing the bluebells I dived underneath and was soon in the clearing. I stood expectantly in front of the gnarly oak wagging my tail.

The outline of Athelstan was dimly visible in the moonlight as he appeared in his usual guise wrapped around the tree.

"Good, good," he said. "We're waiting for you little pup. Come closer to me; I need to tell you a secret."

I stood up on my hind legs and stretched my front legs up the trunk of the mighty tree, trying not to dig in with my claws in case it hurt the gatekeeper. Athelstan bent down his gnarly face and gave me the first of many stories about local history.

He explained that King John had given the land which formed the Common to the citizens of this town of Marlborough in exchange for land more useful to him at the other end of the town nearer to his castle.

In those days the Common was known locally as The Thorns and it provided residents with ample free grazing for their animals, sheep, cows and suchlike. There was a large underground warren which was home to hares and rabbits and these were hunted out with greyhounds as pictured on the town's coat of arms.

He made a harrumphing noise and then whispered 'Quercus' in my ear. The word echoed around and I could smell the wonderful earthy smell of the leaf mould of the forest floor…a heady scent. Athelstan faded once more into the tree. 'What on earth did that mean and what was I supposed to do now?' I wondered.

I sniffed around the tree roots peering through the bluebell leaves, trying to find the hole I had discovered earlier that day. The new growth of the trees rustled in the wind and whispered overhead and they seemed to be saying 'drop the orb….drop the orb' and being a clever little dog I obliged, and immediately lost sight of it. Very concerned as to the whereabouts of my beloved pink ball, I scampered headlong, following its path down a revealed hole, yawning in front of me like a mouth at the bottom of Athelstan's oak tree.

My alert eyes homed in on a faint light coming from the depths of the hole and the first thing I saw were the small folk, Yulia clutching her Da's arm and both were holding up tiny lanterns.

"Come Paddy Paws, follow us; you've opened the time tunnel."

The Secret Adventures of Rolo

Pink ball forgotten, I edged my way along the dark earth tunnel, using my nose to guide me. Yulia kept giggling every time I nudged her with my nose. I couldn't see a thing it was that dark underground and the lantern gave off just a pin prick of light, but for some reason I trusted these little people and pressed blindly on, my sturdy body almost filling the width of the tunnel.

Yulia explained that Da was actually her great great grandfather. He was a wizened little man with a great deal of hair and whiskers. He seemed to know an awful lot about the countryside and nature in general. I found him fascinating. He mumbled away to himself as we felt our way cautiously through the long dark tunnel.

Eventually a stronger glow appeared and as we inched towards it, the light grew ever brighter. The small folk clambered out first, holding aside some brambles to allow me to exit the tunnel. To my surprise it was broad daylight and here we were standing on the edge of a wood looking at some oddly dressed people.

This wasn't a town; certainly not the kind of place the smiley lady and I walk to on a Saturday morning to buy a newspaper. For one thing there were no shops…wait a minute there were no cars nor even any roads and the houses seemed to be small crudely built dwelling places not big brick houses. Where on earth was I?

"We need you to go and fetch something," said Yulia. "We tried to do it ourselves but we are too small for this task so we will wait here to help you find your way back through the time tunnel. You must find a tall man called Peter. Tell him Athelstan sent you and give him the word." They disappeared back into the tunnel entrance. Time tunnel? That was the second time they had mentioned that. What was that all about? I really had no idea.

It then occurred to me that what these miniature people call 'tall' could be anything bigger than themselves, so I had no idea at all where to start.

What was this strange place anyway? I seemed to be in a different time span altogether; certainly not the twenty first century. I needed to ask someone for help and spotted a sleek greyhound stepping carefully over a pile of firewood and leaves rather disdainfully as if he didn't want to get his paws dirty. I thought I would ask him.

The dog towered over me, looked down his long nose rather snootily. He introduced himself as 'De Grys' in a strange sounding accent.
"What on earth are you? I've not seen your sort round here before," he said gruffly peering down his long nose.

"I've been sent to find Peter," I replied, politely sniffing his muzzle and walking around to his rear end in the manner we dogs usually greet each other. The greyhound De Grys walked in a circle so we were face to face again. He stood four square.

"There are many Peters in this village, Peter the Cooper, Peter the Smith, Peter the Thatcher, Peter the Tailor…which Peter are you trying to find?"

I looked down at my paws, feeling rather foolish. I had no idea what he was talking about and said in a small voice, "I don't know what he does but he is supposed to be rather tall."

To my delight the greyhound De Grys replied in a serious tone, "That will probably be Peter Long then…you'll most likely find him out hunting. The people of the hamlet are starving. Food is scarce at the moment. If the hunting party don't find food, the people will go hungry for another day. I'm supposed to be helping them; I'll take you there."

I thanked the snooty hound, trotted along the track behind him; it seemed polite to allow him to go first.

De Grys stopped in a clearing in the woodland. I spied men and women in strange woollen rough spun clothes, carrying cross bows, nets and empty sacks and to my surprise I saw some men holding hawks that appeared to be wearing hoods over their beady eyes. I wondered why the birds weren't allowed to see and asked De Grys. He replied that these birds had been trained to kill pigeons, ducks, geese and partridges and were essential members of the hunting party.

The reason they were kept hooded was so they wouldn't become too excited and go off chasing everything in the woods. When the falconer spotted something worth chasing the hood would be whipped off and only then would the bird be encouraged to seek its prey, kill it and bring it back to its master.

If the prey was too big to carry the bird would stand over it as a marker until it could be retrieved and then it would be rewarded and hooded once more. De Grys himself was used for a different kind of hunting; he and his kind would track deer, rabbits, wild boar and hares. Servants would oversee the chasing dogs, encouraging them to drive the trapped animals into a clearing where hunters would fire arrows to kill the quarry as cleanly as possible and share the meat with the hamlet as a common food larder.

Hares were driven by greyhounds into nets or traps or flushed out of hiding in cornfields and then shot with crossbows. Trouble was food seemed to be a bit scarce at the moment which meant not so many scraps for the dogs. De Grys gave me the impression that he thought he was a very important dog. I kept my thoughts to myself.

A tall man stood out from the gathering. He had a stag draped around his shoulders and he was bowed down by the weight of the carcass, holding its legs together round his neck as he carried it back to the village to portion out the fresh meat amongst the hungry inhabitants. "I would say that's your man; Peter Long," nodded De Grys in the tall man's general direction.

I realised this was my moment and I had to do what I had been sent to do, although I wasn't really sure what that was. I presumed I had to make myself known to Peter Long. I jumped up at the hem of the tall man's coat and he kicked out at me with his buckskin boots, swinging the deer carcass.

"Get away from me you filthy cur," he growled.

Not quite the welcome I was expecting. Perhaps he thought I was trying to steal his food. I had to think of another way of getting his attention. Then I had an idea.

Knowing that this party were foraging for food and that we terriers are expert hunters (my smiley lady said so), I thought I could help.

Although they had venison for their supper that night, I reckoned one deer wouldn't go far amongst this large gathering of hungry people. Remembering Athelstan's history lesson about the warren beneath the Common, it occurred to me that these people might not know of the underground larder; they had yet to discover it for themselves.

I thought that we were not far from the location of the warren and I disappeared in the undergrowth, unnoticed by the hunting party who were gathering around the bearer of tonight's supper. I found my way to the Common and located the warren by means of following my nose. I sniffed out the nearest rabbit hole; bolted down it and brought up a sleeping rabbit. I carried it back in my jaws and laid it on the path. De Grys was at my side now,

"How on earth did you learn how to do that?" the greyhound asked, clearly impressed.

"It's in the genes," I said with as much of an air of importance as I could muster. Then I bade the snooty greyhound follow me so I could show him where the source of food could be found. I shot back in the undergrowth to find the hole again and came back with another rabbit.

It seemed clear to me that this greyhound wouldn't fit down any hole. Even though he had long legs, he was only good for chasing not for fetching nor retrieving and certainly not for digging. I could actually bring them from their burrows because Athelstan had told me something that these people had yet to discover: where to find the rabbits. Now I had shared the secret with De Grys – he could at least show Peter Long and the others where to hunt. When I'd repeated this exercise several times, we took up five rabbits and went back to the others and laid them in a line at the tall man's feet. I then plucked up the courage to speak to him again,

"Excuse me, sir, if you are Peter Long, I come with a message from Athelstan." The tall man stopped in his tracks and bent down to inspect me more closely.

"Goodness! You're a strange messenger and no mistake!" he exclaimed, peering at me. He picked me up by the scruff of my neck and inspected me more closely. He had a long nose like the greyhound. and was very rude, I thought.

"We could do with you around here. A dog of your

size could be useful. Want to stay? You could share hearth space and scraps with De Grys here in return for your hunting skills."

I shook my head politely and repeated the word I had been given by Athelstan 'Quercus' and was surprised to find it seemed to have the desired effect. He set me down on my feet.

The big man known as Peter Long fished in his pocket and brought out a small silver coin with the word 'Maerleber' printed on it.

"How the devil are you going to carry this?" he muttered. Then he pulled a piece of cloth from his pocket, wrapped it round the coin tightly and bent down to tuck the small bundle under my collar for safe keeping, smacking me on the rump as if I were a horse.
"Off you go then."

I bade farewell to De Grys, and hoped I hadn't offended him by turning down the offer of forming a partnership and staying with these hunting folk. The snooty greyhound stood wistfully watching as I trotted off in the direction of the woodland where I had left Yulia and her Da. I had done my duty here: shown the people where the rabbit warren was, and collected Athelstan's coin in payment. What an adventure!

Sure enough the little folk were waiting anxiously by the tunnel entrance, tiny lanterns still aflame, peering out and awaiting my return.

"Did you get it?" asked the tiny old man, gruffly. Yulia saw the bundle under my collar and she motioned towards the hole in the bank.

"That was Athelstan's test to see if you are worthy of Understory adventures. If it went well, we will be seeing a lot more of each other as you could prove very useful, Paddy Paws. Get the coin to Athelstan and then yourself off home before dawn breaks or you will be missed!" she said, leading the way back down the tunnel.

The Secret Adventures of Rolo

I didn't know what she was talking about but that was the second time I had been told I could prove useful. I wagged my tail in approval of the praise. Blinking in the early morning light as I clambered out from the tunnel, I gave myself a good shake and took in the familiarity of the smell of the undergrowth at the foot of the oak tree.

Athelstan slowly appeared in front of me, in his usual guise, wrapped around the tree trunk, camouflaged by the woody bark.

"Good, good, little pup. I was right in my choice; I knew you were worthy," and with that he unfurled a claw, reached down and carefully took the tiny cloth bundle from my collar and shook out the silver coin. He tucked the material back under my collar for safe keeping.

"Don't forget to take the orb," Athelstan whispered as he faded back into the bark. Orb? No idea what that was but I spied the pink ball exactly where it had fallen at the beginning of the adventure and so I

picked it up and carried it in my mouth.
Without further ado I trotted back towards the
bushes that led to the other, less magical side of
the wood. I glanced back over my shoulder and to
my surprise the hole in the bottom of the tree had
closed up. Perhaps I had imagined it all! I ran home
as fast as I could, along the footpath, back under the
gate, up the garden steps past the secret inhabitant
and through the trapdoor, bursting out from under
the sink and onto the kitchen floor, knocking over
the cleaning products in my haste.

I kicked the cupboard door shut with my back legs
and had just settled down in my basket when I heard
the kitchen door open and the smiley lady came in
wearing her snuggly dressing gown and she rubbed
my tummy and let me out for my early morning
wee.

I obliged and came back in for a biscuit and then
snuggled back into my basket.

"How strange!" she said, picking up the piece of

57

folded material.

"Where on earth did this come from? Anyone would think you'd been out all night you sleepyhead Rolo, don't you want to go walkies?" she teased as she jangled my lead.

The Secret Adventures of Rolo

Chapter 5

Understory Adventure – Rolo and The English Civil War

And so my life had changed yet again…from fourth-hand rescue pup to a good pet, safe and secure in a loving home, and now it seemed I was some kind of forest gatekeeper's night time messenger! By day I am exhausted and my people can't figure out why… I have to fit in my blogging when the others aren't around to see what I'm up to. They have no idea how clever is the rescue dog they have welcomed into their home!

Dog blog #2 According to Rolo

```
Having promised to blog, I'm sorry
I just haven't had time lately.
Also I have to be really careful
that my people don't see what I'm
up to. The boy with the floppy hair
throws his stuff down in the hallway
```

when he comes home from school and complains that I'm too worn out when he wants to play with me.

Just as well I don't eat shoes; I could have a field day with all his Size 8s left around the front door. I want to please him and I jump on his lap a lot and lick his chin. This is all a ploy as I now know his password and can use his laptop whenever I want! He doesn't take me out very often — it's usually the smiley lady. She says he's lazy.

However, he is playing cricket this evening and the lady says we're going to watch and maybe I can be an outfielder. No one's thrown a ball for me yet. I guess we'll get to that. I always keep my pink ball at home in the daytime as I don't want to lose it. The rules of cricket seem a bit complicated to me...what's all this 'in' and 'out' and 'silly mid-off' stuff? The wicket looks to be a useful peeing post to me.

Oops, suddenly I find I've been banished to sit in the car. I'm beginning to learn to do as I'm told and respond to my name — unless I'm following an exciting 'scent' of course — then I have

The Secret Adventures of Rolo

selective hearing. The smiley lady gets cross but forgives me as she thinks I've not really had any formal training before.

I think she understands me. I have come to understand that I am not allowed upstairs. The lady has piled some boxes at the bottom of the stairs and it's quite comical watching her climb over them especially carrying a laptop or a cup of tea. I wish I could go in their bedrooms; I'd be very cute to cuddle up to in bed but the smiley lady is adamant that I stay downstairs, despite the floppy haired boy's pleadings.

By the way, he has noticed that I do something which he calls 'clown eyes.'
He thinks I do it to look cute or

to beg for a share of something he
is eating, but actually it happens
when I'm having visions. Not
flashbacks; visions; things that I
am about to see.

When my eyes close into little
slits, which appear to open
vertically rather than horizontally
(hence 'clown eyes'), I am seeing
things I will soon witness on
my night time adventures. How
impressed would the boy be if
he knew that?! Today I dreamt of
balls, not to chase but rather to
dodge. Whatever could that mean?

Tucked up in bed again at night, I am once more
summoned by the owl and its tiny rider. Back
through the under sink trapdoor and out into the
night; down the steps (no time now to sniff at the
mysterious inhabitant of the decking) and squeeze
under the gate; on and on: through the wood, under

the bushes and at last at the base of the mighty oak waiting for Athelstan to speak.

"Same place?" I ask Yulia as we once more enter the dark tunnel, having left the pink ball at its entrance.

"Not this time Paddy Paws, a different place entirely," she smiled. Something had been puzzling me and I thought this might be a good time to mention it. I asked Yulia if she knew why the secret place was called the Understory.

"That's easy!" she replied. "It's because there are several layers to the forest. The 'canopy' refers to the topmost branches of the trees, and the bottom part, where the tree roots are and where we small folk live, is called the 'Understory' - it's as simple as that. Nothing to tell you about this journey; you will know what you have to do when you get there." Her Da smiled his toothless smile and muttered "good gal, you do listen!" and without further ado they escorted me through the time tunnel and eventually towards daylight where Yulia bade me farewell and

'Godspeed', whatever that might be.

Here is Da's wisdom for the month of June, as told to me to pass the time on the journey through the time tunnel as I follow their tiny lanterns. I think it is Da's mission to educate me in the ways of nature.

June: "A leak in June brings harvest soon."

The tune of June is the humming of a great bee chorus; these industrious winged soldiers are so busy at this time of year collecting nectar wherever they find bright flowers. Nettles are in bloom, wild briar roses peep through the hedgerows and the elder is on the turn.

Old folk lore says: 'summer is not here until the elder flowers, and summer ends when the berries are ripe.' Honeysuckle scent is heady in the evening and water lilies grace ponds.

Forget—me—nots fill the banks of streams

and purple loosestrife grows tall. This
is the month when conifers show fresh
growth; holly has bright new leaves. There
is less bird song in the air, it's as if the
robin and thrush have lost their voices,
although warblers whistle a pretty tune.
Young birds are learning to fly and the
strain of parenting and losing their feathers
(moulting) keeps parents a little subdued.
This is the time for tadpoles of newts,

frogs and toads to be spied by the keen-
eyed in the streams and ponds, and fish

can be seen emerging to snap up may-flies
that dance too closely to the surface of
the water. Dragon flies flash their jewelled
bodies as they skim the watery surface
in the sunshine. Look out for the first
tortoiseshell butterfly, stretching its wings
on a warm brick wall.

This time I recognised the Common when I crawled
out from the tunnel. Again it seemed as if I had
gone back in time. Not more rabbit hunting! I know
where to find them though…this is the same place
as my last adventure. No sign of De Grys and Peter
Long; perhaps this was a different time.

I could see earthworks presumably dug to defend
something, and tents flapping in the breeze and
all manner of people milling around; mainly men
dressed in rough woollen clothing, doublet and hose
and some were wearing metal armour in the form of
breastplates and heavy helmets. The colour of their
clothing was dull and dreary. The men appeared
to be at ease; some were sharpening swords, or

servicing weapons, gathered in clusters around small fires. This was either after a battle, or judging by the lack of wounded, perhaps before one. The men were talking as they worked at their tasks and I edged closer unobserved and lifted an ear, all the better for listening:

"The castle won't give. Lord Seymour is holding it for the King…but the Town is with us," said one of the burly men as he gave his blade an extra polish, holding it up to the sky to admire his handiwork as it glinted in the sunlight.

"Where is the King anyways?" asked another man who was cleaning his musket with an oily rag, spitting on it to add polish to the wood and metal.

"Not round these parts…he wouldn't be welcome here," replied the sword polisher, satisfied with his work and sheathing his sword in his belt.
"I've heard he's in Oxford not so far from here," piped up another soldier.

I scurried off before I was noticed. It appeared
that I was in a Roundhead encampment in the
Seventeenth Century. Why on earth had Athelstan
sent me here I wondered, and who was I supposed
to be helping?

I trotted away from the camp where they didn't
look too friendly, and scampered down an alleyway
which led to a church. Suddenly shots rang out – it
seemed that musket balls were actually being fired at
the church tower! I ducked into the porch and there
I met a young lad, much younger than my floppy
haired boy, but he seemed friendly enough and as
we were sheltering together, I nuzzled his dirty bare
leg and he stroked my ears.

He introduced himself as Walter. I told him my
name. He didn't seem at all surprised to be talking
to a dog. Such was the innocence of the young. He
said he had a very important message for Colonel
James Ramsey, the commander of the Army up on
the Common.

"I've read some of the letter," he said proudly,

unfolding the piece of paper and tracing the writing with his finger as if proving that he could read, as if I might doubt his word.

"It says that Lord Digby is on his way with an army of men loyal to the King and he will demand the surrender of this rebel town."

Crikey, I thought, I seemed to have stumbled upon some sort of battle; turns out it's the English Civil War! Walter was saying he'd better get back up on the Common and deliver the message pretty sharpish. I asked the lad if he knew the date and he said it was 23rd November in the year of 1642.

I wondered how Walter would get near the commander of the Roundheads and thought I'd tag along in case I could be of assistance. We ran up the alley way together and once more skirted the fires until we came to an impressive looking tent which Walter thought must belong to Colonel James Ramsey.

Walter asked one of the wandering soldiers and they confirmed this was the right tent. Only one problem: two guards with giant pike staffs at least eighteen feet long with spikes on the end and crossed like a barrier stood at the entrance; our way was barred.

Whilst Walter stated his business, I could see that he wasn't going to get past these two burly guards standing there like bookends so whilst he was waving the letter about and explaining his task, I jumped up, snatched it from his hand and darted under a tent flap before anyone realised what was going on and could stop me.

Expecting to find myself being hauled up by the collar at any moment I was surprised to find myself inside the tent. It smelt musty and masculine and of squashed grass, mud and canvas.
This was campaign headquarters.

A group of men were sat around the table arguing over a map. It seemed that Marlborough was important to the King because of its geographic

71

location between London and Bristol and closeness to Oxford. The King didn't like the town's defiance and was afraid that others nearby would follow suit. I had to deliver the letter and without thinking things through, and and much to his alarm, I jumped on the lap of the man at the head of the table, assuming him to be the boss.

"What the…" then he saw the folded paper sticking out of my mouth and he took hold of it in his big hands, easing it out and opening the message carefully, smoothing it on the table.

"Brave pup," said Colonel James Ramsay when he had read the letter's contents and I jumped down quickly. The big man threw me a piece of meat from a piled platter in front of him.

I snuck back out from the tent and hid around the earthworks. Walter was nowhere to be seen. I watched as messengers were sent scurrying down into the town on horseback, presumably carrying the news of the impending invasion. I figured it was time to scamper back down the time tunnel and run home; my work here was done.

I found out the rest of the story from Athelstan later:

The next day, when Lord Digby rode into Marlborough at the head of a four hundred strong cavalry, he was repelled by the townsfolk because they had been forewarned of the Royalists' plan. He regrouped his army and returned on 5th December with ten times that number in his army and this time the townsfolk were powerless to stand against the Royalists though they fought bravely to the last.

After three days of bitter siege the King's men overran the earthworks on the Common and ransacked the town, riding skirmishes down the alleyways, still under musket fire from windows of the town houses in the High Street.

Luckily the townsfolk were expecting the attack and were able to hide their treasures and board up their properties to protect themselves as much as they could, but even so their more than fifty homes and several barns were put to the torch and others looted to the Royalist cry of 'A town for the King!'.

One hundred and twenty Roundhead soldiers were rounded up and marched as prisoners of the King to Oxford; but despite this defeat, Cromwell, the Commander in Chief of the Roundheads' never forgot the bravery of the town. Athelstan added that Cromwell and the people of Marlborough owed a great debt of gratitude to the little rescue dog who had delivered the important warning on the eve of the battle, as things could have gone a lot worse.

Chapter 6

Understory Adventure – Rolo and The Fire of Marlborough

Da's folklore wisdom for July: "St Swithun's Day (15th July) if thou dost rain for forty days it will remain. St Swithun's Day if thou be fair, for forty days 'twill rain no more."

This is the month when you can inhale the best fragrance in the world simply by getting out into the countryside and taking a deep breath: warm, intoxicating, and heady, nothing beats the scent of freshly cut grass. If only we could bottle it and take it out to revive our spirits in winter.

Along the hedgerows, brambles are in white flower (a sure sign of a good blackberry crop to come). Hollyhocks, sunflowers and clematis are on full showy display in

gardens. Light green cereal crops in the
fields, such as oats and barley and wheat
turn a darker colour as they swell.
Swifts scream overhead as they swoop
low, and starlings begin to flock. This is the
time when nesting is nearly over. The tall elm
trees offer shade and in the late afternoon
the shadows stretch long and lean on the
ground.

Blue scabious and harebell flowers reflect
the blue of the summer sky growing on the
chalk downs. Fox glove and willow herb, both
tall and pink, tower loftily over woodland
dells. Lime trees give off their distinctive

delicious scent (nothing to do with citrus fruit, a different type of lime) and insects love it.

Keen-eyed nature watchers might spy glow worms lighting their lamps in hedgerows at night and you may be lucky to see any kind of owl gliding on silent wings through the moonlight on a hunting mission; or even a nightjar. Look out too for the stunning and showy red admiral and peacock butterflies in the warm sunshine.

Dog blog #3 According to Rolo

Me again. Just got a moment to myself whilst the smiley lady is picking the floppy haired boy up from the skate park. Boy am I tired...dog tired! What a double life I lead! I'd hardly been in my basket five minutes when the smiley lady woke me at four o'clock in the morning; much earlier than usual. She let me out in the garden for 5 minutes run around, begging me to keep quiet and not wake the neighbours, and then she shut me back in the kitchen.

Phew - back to bed then - I need a lot more sleep. How could she have known I'd only been in my basket for less than half an hour before she let me out? If she'd come down any earlier she would have found an empty basket!

The smiley lady was apparently doing an 'airport run' whatever that is - I don't think it's some kind of exciting and energetic aerobic exercise and anyway I wasn't invited. The half-asleep floppy haired boy slipped my lead on at a more respectable seven o'clock

and took me out for a walk and a
whizz and gave me breakfast before
he went off to school — that's a
first; he rarely takes me out! We'd
just reached the top of the drive
on our way home when the smiley
lady's car pulled in and out jumped
a very bubbly red head - (no not a
Red Setter dog; another lady). She
didn't know whether to greet me or
the floppy haired boy first — he got
2 air kisses and I just got ruffled
and patted.

I gather from the smiley lady we
will see her for lots of jolly
walks in the summer. She has a
Jack Russell of her own who is old
enough to be my doggy granddad.
Alas he lives in a faraway hot
place, but I can tell this jolly
lady likes me and she is in the
area for the duration of the summer

holidays. I'm such an endearing pup; I can win most people round with my charm it seems! Oops, I can hear the car on the drive. Better sign off.

Dog blog #4 According to Rolo

A car journey and a lovely walk through swishy grass and mud afterwards - and a new and very enclosed garden to explore. The birds in the hedges are a bit bloomin' noisy though — I really don't know why they keep shrieking when I stand on my back legs and peer through the leaves. Followed some deer tracks and nearly had a pesky grey squirrel!

Nodded off in the car in my little pop up tent on the back seat on the way home and would have continued

sleeping but the smiley lady opened
the patio door and I saw arch enemy
number one; next door's cat in MY
garden. Had to see it off, even if
I did trample all over the lady's
newly planted lettuce seedlings
in my pursuit and flattened the
silly little border fence of her
poor attempt at creating an alpine
garden.

At least the pesky cat disappeared
over the fence. I'll get it next
time. There is definitely still
something undiscovered lurking
under the decking. I KNOW YOU ARE
THERE AND I WILL FIND YOU!

Dog blog #5 According to Rolo

They're out in the garden so I've
got a few minutes to put paw to
keyboard. Well I've been in my new

home for a while now (I've lost count of the days) and yesterday the manager of Dogs Trust rang to see how I was getting on. I heard the floppy haired boy say I was a good boy but he wouldn't let me speak to them.

Some funny things happened this week. The lady took me for a nice walk down to Town and up on the Common via a narrow lane. We had to walk on the road as there was no pavement and she kept me on a short lead.

The lady heard a van coming up the road so she held me tightly and made me sit at her feet, tucked into the bank. The sound of the engine came closer and closer but still we couldn't see it. I realised long before the lady did, that it was in fact a tractor behind the hedge running parallel to the road. I decided to humour her. She cottoned on eventually and could be heard chuckling to herself.

The smiley lady and the boy played 'fetch' with me indoors in the hallway as it was raining. They seemed surprised that I knew 'fetch' and 'drop'- of course I do! But it's not their fault, they don't know about Athelstan and that I'm a Very Important Secret Messenger!

When it stopped raining, the lady and the boy took me over the road and up on the green and threw a tennis ball for me. Well, it was way too exciting out there to chase a silly ball, so I ran round and

The Secret Adventures of Rolo

round in circles and kept coming back to them. Then it started raining again and we came home. They seemed pleased with my good behaviour. I was towel dried on the recycling box in the porch within an inch of my life, and firmly brushed. The lady said I smelt of 'damp dog'.

The next day the smiley lady and her friend took me for a really long walk up on the downs and I was off the lead for about an hour. I watched them out from the corner of my eye and when we got to long grass… well… that's the only time you'll catch me walking closely to heel.

I couldn't see over the tall stalks — it was all a bit swishy swashy and rather scary. I had a lovely time running along hedgerows and came back when they called me — I never let them get too far ahead — even when they hid from me I found them...well you have to humour them! When the floppy haired boy came home from school he took me over to the field with a tennis ball launcher. He let me off the lead and was really really cross when I ran all the way home, down the alley way and even across the road. I thought I was really clever and just showing him that I knew where I lived.

I was told off big time and ignored for a bit. I seemed to have blotted my copybook. Later that evening, the smiley lady took me up on the green and let me off the lead. I remembered seeing 2 black flat cats with twinkling eyes on the front lawn guarding a house near the alley way leading to the green.

I ran as fast as I could and knocked over one of the cats — amazing — it fell right over and just lay there with its eyes glinting in the grass! Then I ran and hid behind a bush. The lady caught up with me and was very cross indeed. I bet the owners of the house are wondering why one of their ornamental cats has been uprooted and is lying face down on the grass.

Course I knew they weren't real…I was just pretending. Anyway I got put to bed very firmly and told off for running away - twice - not sure when I'll be let off the lead again but am thinking it won't be on the green for a while. Got to go now.

Byeeeee.

The floppy haired boy wasn't feeling too well today and stayed home from school. I snuggled up to him on the sofa and kept him warm. Time to catch up on some much needed sleep.

The floppy haired boy said I was doing 'clown eyes' and for some reason I couldn't get 'cats' out of my mind as I drifted off to sleep finally tucked up in my basket for the night…zzzz…I thought it might be something to do with the silly flat cats. Then I awoke to the familiar tap tap tap at the window…Yulia was beckoning me from her owl perch.

"Can I ask you Yulia and Da, does this tunnel always lead to the same place? I always seem to be up on the Common."

"No, not always," replied Yulia. "It is a time tunnel and can cover huge distances as well as different eras." I was not really sure how that would work but who was I to question? I was just enjoying the

87

adventure and excitement of being 'the chosen one'!

Well, I seemed to be up on the Common again for the third time but thankfully in peace time. There was a great commotion coming from half way down the hill, a great deal of red light glowing in the sky; it looked as if the town was on fire. Without stopping to think what time frame I was in, I ran instinctively as fast as I could towards the smoke and flames.

The town of Marlborough was indeed engulfed by fire and the townspeople, no longer divided by civil war, were trying to organise human bucket chains to quench the roaring flames. Most of the houses and shops were not only thatched but joined together along the street so the fire easily spread from house to house, swallowing up everything in its path, completely unchecked. I heard someone say the fire had started in the tannery at the Castle end of the town.

A man in authority was trying to explain that the best way to stop the spread of the fire was to pull down a building further along the high street so as to break the 'fuse' and give the rescuers a chance to get ahead and better manage the quenching of the blaze. Eventually the man got his message across. A gang of townsfolk picked up rakes and pitchforks and improvised in any way they could, dragging the straw down from a roof further along the road, causing the fire to stop in its tracks, rage for a moment and wonder where to go next.

This gave the rescuers a chance to dowse the flames and get ahead of the path of the fire. It was dangerous and hot work and the people fought tirelessly against the flames to demolish the house before it too was engulfed. Meanwhile the owner and his wife comforted each other, standing in the street, not quite believing what was happening to their property. It seemed their house had to be sacrificed in order for the rest of the town to be saved.

I was unsure how I could help; and then looked towards where people were pointing and shouting

and I saw smoke pouring out from the tower of St
Mary's church at the other end of the town, half
way back up the hill towards the common. Surely
the whole town was now ablaze! Without hesitating
I raced towards the blazing church, took a deep
lungful of air and pushed open the heavy oak door
with my nose, worried in case anyone was taking
refuge inside.

The church was historically a place of sanctuary but
at this moment in time the worst place anyone could
hide trying to flee the fire. The stone building itself
appeared thankfully empty - everyone was probably
fighting the fire down in the town - but the roof had
caught alight and the interior was burning.

The whole place was full of thick black smoke.
About to leave, I heard a horrible panicking mewing
sound and peering under one of the pews by the
vestry I spied the church cat, who prized itself on
being a fine mouser huddling with her litter of
kittens. She hissed a warning when she saw me. No
time for dog and cat chase games now, I thought...

all my instincts told me to help her.

There were four kittens to be rescued and the smoke was choking and the chances of the mother cat's rescue efforts being successful were slim. I barked angrily at the cat, trying to let her know I was boss and she was to listen and that I could help her move the terrified kittens. This was no time for fighting. She eyed me warily, then snatched up a kitten by the scruff of its neck in her mouth and motioned to me, by softening her angry glare, to do the same.

The kitten squealed as I opened by mouth but I carried it very gently without clamping my jaws too tightly, and deposited it at the mother cat's feet in the church porch away from the raging inferno inside. I took another deep breath of fresh air and plunged back into the smoke filled interior, mother cat close behind me.

We seized the last two kittens by the same means and scampered quickly down the main aisle, turning only when we heard an almighty crash as a burning lintel fell in the chancel and landed exactly where the cat family had been hiding, smashing the pew. We gained the porch and mother cat set to work cleaning up her squeaking offspring. All were safe for now. The roof was all but burned down and the internal structure was also in flames, luckily the stone withheld the flames.

"You can't stay here," I warned, and once more helped her move the family to the relative safety of the old yew tree in the churchyard just across

from the west door. The tree was hollow inside and offered great sanctuary and soon the kittens were snuggled down within the tree to see out the catastrophe.

"How can I ever thank you for saving my family?" asked the mother cat and I smiled and explained that dogs would always chase cats - it's in our nature - but that I was happy to have helped with the rescue and I'd be sure to remember her if I met her again on one of my adventures.

She didn't understand what I was talking about, so I left her calming her kittens and went back to the time tunnel, noticing that the sky above the town was less red, the fire presumably under control.

Retelling the story to Athelstan as I emerged from the base of his tree in the moonlight, he laughed and said I had to go and look at the stone carving on the eaves next to St Mary's Church tower. He wouldn't be drawn to tell me anything else about what he meant, so I would have to wait until the smiley lady or the floppy haired boy took me to that end of the High Street.

Athelstan did tell me, though, that during the great fire of Marlborough, within just three hours,

some 250 houses were destroyed and thereafter
no more thatched roofs were allowed in the town.
Oliver Cromwell, by now Lord Protector, true to his
word about rewarding the loyal Roundhead town
from the Civil War, commissioned the rebuilding
of Marlborough in 1653 by means of compulsory
national subscription.

This is why The Merchant's House in the High Street
survives in such good condition to this day, now
lovingly cared for by volunteer townspeople who are
very proud of its history.

I scampered home, tired out from the adventure and
too much smoke inhalation and fell exhausted into
bed just before I was woken to embrace the new day.

The smiley lady sniffed me suspiciously and, without
standing on ceremony, dropped me in a sink full of
warm bubbly water. I don't mind a bath. I was put
out in the conservatory to dry in the warmth of the
sun through the glass. I slept, of course, as you knew
I would. Life is pretty good.

Chapter 7

Understory Adventure – Rolo and the Invention of Catseyes

"Where am I off to this time then Yulia?" I asked the tiny woodland person as I approached the foot of the oak tree. She was waiting for me, lantern already lit and held aloft. We watched the owl together as it flew off over the tree tops, no doubt looking for a midnight snack on its way home.

I asked Yulia where her winged taxi lived and she said she would show me the tree. His family had been nesting in the same hole in a bough for at least twenty years. Athelstan materialised and spoke at once:

"You're going to witness the birth of an invention," was all the gatekeeper would say, rather mysteriously. Yulia and her Da lit my way down the hole as usual and I followed her tiny lantern silently, wondering what adventure the night would bring.

95

Emerging from the tunnel, I found myself in a very bleak place. It certainly wasn't the Common. The air felt very cold and surely more northerly in location than Wiltshire. No idea what year it was - there didn't seem to be any sign of weapons or machinery this time. It was very dark - and foggy too, and with the fog came the smell of damp. I seemed to be smack in the middle of nowhere - certainly not in a town - somewhere out in the countryside, I thought.

There was a road - a very windy road with no traffic on it and then I spied a metal sign which pointed with a finger one way to Bradford and the opposite way to Halifax. What on earth was I doing here? I wondered. What invention was I about to witness? Suddenly I saw an arch enemy; yes, a CAT, strolling as casually as you like, down the side of the road, daintily up on its tiptoes like it owned the place. This was like a red rag to a bull!

I chased it across the road and it almost fell down the side of a gorge. I lay off my chasing to allow it to regain a foothold. I had a sense of fair play after all.

Then I looked down and my life flashed before me
- we were poised on the side of a very steep valley
which had been hidden in the blanket of the fog!
The cat and I could have tumbled together to certain
death mid fight! The cat was now sitting very still on
the side of the road on a very sharp bend, unaware
of the danger, pretending to be invisible.

I had a sense of déjà-vu and thought for a moment
I recognised the cat. No, it couldn't be. I couldn't
be bothered to chase it – not when there was
such a dangerous drop on the other side. I spied a
triangular road sign with a red border, warning of
the bend but it didn't seem very visible to motorists
in this weather.

Then I heard a car engine; a bit spluttery; the
sound dulled by the swirling fog, and then a vehicle
appeared out of the gloom as if by magic; not a
modern day car like the smiley lady drives, but
a very old fashioned kind of open topped motor,
being driven very slowly and carefully by a man in
a big coat and wearing a flat cap pulled down on his

head. I could hear him muttering to his companion
through the scarf which muffled his voice as he

drove the car at snail's pace along the foggy road.
He seemed to be banging on about the Corporation
having removed the tram lines for repair which
meant there was nothing to follow on the road in the
dark, and therefore adding to the hazard of driving
on the perilously winding road in the fog.

I glanced over at the cat, as it looked as if it was

thinking about bolting in front of the car to get away from me. I hissed at it from under my breath and told it that I wouldn't harm it and to stay very still. Hurrah! It seemed to be listening to me and its eyes shone brightly, yellow dots picked up by the headlamps of the rattly old car. Then the driver did something extraordinary.

He stopped the car suddenly, pulled on the handbrake, pushed back his cap, scratched his head and then thumped on the steering wheel as if he'd just had a brainwave. He started explaining something at length to his companion, waving his arms about and pointing to the static cat.

The cat stood very still indeed, mesmerised by the headlamps and not even blinking. Now I don't know much about the ancestry of cats, or how much they move about and change territory down the years, but if I were a gambling dog I would put money on this one being related to the mother cat from the Marlborough Fire. There was something about it and I'm sure it recognised me too. That's all I'm saying. The driver was Percy Shaw and the year was 1933.

I had just witnessed this Yorkshire man dreaming up the idea of the motoring aid 'catseyes': light -reflecting studs set down into the road surface to illuminate the middle of the road to mark out the lanes for night time traffic, powered not by electricity but by the cars' own headlamps.

This invention would go on to make Percy Shaw a very rich man and save millions of lives not only in England but all over the world. Shaw spent a few years perfecting and patenting his design, sinking the reflective glass spheres in rubber casing which cushioned the 'eye' if a wheel drove over it.

He even had the brainwave to mount these rubber mats into a cast iron base which collected rainwater naturally and so the 'catseye' studs, when squashed down, would wash themselves clean in a process similar to the function of the human tear when someone is blinking.

Impressed, I made my way carefully through the fog to the tunnel entrance, where Yulia carrying her tiny lantern was anxiously waiting. Da had already gone home being thoroughly cold and damp and quite grumpy. I told Yulia about the cat and its reflective eyes and that I thought I recognised the cat from my previous adventure.

I said if I'd got to the scene a bit earlier, Shaw's invention may have been called 'Dog's Eyes' and I would have become famous....anyway I'll look at those ornamental flat cats with their beady eyes standing on the neighbours front lawn in a completely different light now - I'd just witnessed the discovery of the motorist's friend: real 'catseyes'!

Dog blog #6 According to Rolo

Me again. The laptop is left in hibernation mode so I'm seizing the opportunity to update you. Saturday was quite a dry day and I had some lovely walks, quite confidently off the lead now of course, scampering over the fields towards some farmland. Crossing the wheat field I always stay at my smiley lady's heel because I can't see over the swishy swashy long green stuff and it's very scary, not that I'll tell them that of course. Other than that, I'm always out in front of my people with my white flag of a tail flying, and I nearly always come back when called.

Funnily enough, they always put me back on the lead before I have a chance to bolt down the alley from the field and flatten the other metal cat (by the way the other one is still lying face down on the grass!). I merely nod to the flat cats with their shiny eyes since my last adventure!

Just when I thought I'd had all my exercise for the day, it started

raining, seriously raining - cats
and dogs they said - not that I saw
any, just a lot of water.

I was surprised to find myself on
the lead and out the front door
again later that day, down to
Manton and a big field for a concert
called Mantonfest. My smiley lady
was saying it was a marvellous
community event to raise money for
the new village hall; and people
turned out to see the many local
performers, despite the inclement
weather and soggy field.

At 7pm the Community Choir
enthusiastically took to the stage
and I watched the smiley lady and
others in red t-shirts sing. I
decided not to join in as I didn't
think it was quite the done thing,
and I did enjoy my first festival,

103

despite the mud. Other people kept feeding me bits of burger under their chairs so all in all it was quite good fun even though I was firmly tethered to a chair leg. We were in a marquee so as not to get too wet.

The choir in red t-shirts were drinking from big glasses some kind of brown liquid - didn't look too good to me - but they were all laughing and singing noisily.

On Sunday I had a paddle and a drink from the River Kennet and discovered I quite like water. Next day I went in for a swim (or, perhaps more accurately, as you might expect, a doggy paddle). Oops, I can hear a flurry of activity. All for now - more later. Back again… Rolo here.

This morning was quite exciting as the smiley lady took me to meet up with her jolly friend and they were having a good old chinwag as we walked along the towpath. At Devizes, I saw a couple of men in canoes and thought I would race them. I ran as fast as I could along the towpath, under the bridge and out of sight, and then I just couldn't help myself.

I decided to jump in for a swim to cool down. Afterwards, my lady told me off because she was secretly panicking about me not being able to get out again, as the sides of the canal were so steep and she didn't want to have to plunge into the canal to save me.

Casual as you like, I pulled myself up the sheer bank and had a good shake dry. (She was visualising ringing Dogs Trust and saying 'can I have another dog please, I've lost this one.') No harm done, though I'll probably do it again if I can get away with it.

Hmmmmm, an ominous looking parcel has just arrived on the doorstep delivered by a white van; not the usual postman in red with his reflective jacket.I have a feeling this delivery is something to do with me.

The smiley lady is waiting for the floppy haired boy to come home from school to fix it in place. The suspicious flat pack is propped up against the boxes at the bottom of the stairs. Watch this space… gotta go now.

Dog blog #7 According to Rolo

Hello again!
I love cricket! The smiley lady doesn't let me off the lead at the ground but I sit quietly next to her on the grass and watch 22 floppy haired boys in their whites and listen to the thwack of leather on willow. Lovely summer pastime!

I can even pick out my boy when he's got a borrowed helmet and pads on despite all 22 of them looking the same! The only time I barked in two and a half hours was when a golden retriever started playing with a frisbee on the far side of the pitch - I sooooo wanted to join in, but the smiley lady wouldn't let me off the lead.

Meanie! Instead she took me for a

The Secret Adventures of Rolo

walk behind the sight screen so I couldn't see the frisbee and the umpire was heard to tut loudly about the noisy dog. Who was that then?

When we got home there was some serious construction going on. **Now** I know what was in the big box:a stair gate. The smiley lady is pleased as she doesn't have to climb over boxes of books anymore. I thought it must be to stop the floppy haired boy coming down to raid the fridge, but no, it's for my benefit apparently.

For some reason they don't want me going upstairs. More tomorrow, when I can get on the laptop unobserved...

I'm back.

The Secret Adventures of Rolo

This morning I sat in the car for a couple of hours listening to Radio 2 (I like Pop Master) whilst the smiley lady took me to visit her dad (known to me and the floppy haired boy as 'granddad').

She took him dinner in a basket. It wasn't dog food and there was none for me, and I'm not allowed to beg. She took my brown blanket so I knew we were going to sit quietly for a while. I thought it would be impolite to sniff round the flat, so I was a very good boy and even sat on granddad's lap for a cuddle.

He said he was very pleased to meet me. The smiley lady says we will visit him again next week. Better than being left at home. I like older people as they are calm; I feel very protective of granddad.

There was a great big Common to explore (no Roundhead encampments!) and the smiley lady said she used to play there when she was a puppy. I dug a big hole in the grass. Can't really explain why… I like digging, though it makes my paws muddy.

I am a champion digger. I came back when the smiley lady called me because I know where my bread is buttered. She stomped the turf back down where I'd been digging. Didn't find anything — just practising. Who knows when I might need my digging skills? Then the long drive home and more Radio 2 this time

The Secret Adventures of Rolo

listening to 'Non-Stop Oldies' with the smiley lady singing along. Tomorrow I am apparently meeting another Nanny and Granddad.

"Not so far to drive," the smiley lady said.

The floppy haired boy came in from school and ignored me, immediately reaching for his laptop. I wasn't having any of that so I lay across the keyboard and made him laugh till he finally got the message and rubbed my tummy. He said I was doing 'clown eyes' - I was thinking about digging holes.

Chapter 8

Understory Adventure – Rolo Discovers Crop Rotation

I could hardly wait to go to bed these past few days. After the kitchen door was shut and I was tucked in goodnight and told to 'be a good boy', I would listen for the creak of the stairs, the flushing of the loo and the banging of bedroom doors and for the household to go quiet, which let me know that the inhabitants had gone to bed.

I kicked off my blanket, found my pink ball (as it seemed to be a very necessary key to these adventures) and trot over to the kitchen cupboard under the sink, paw the door open, squeeze through the cleaning paraphernalia and pull open the trapdoor, minding my very wobbly tooth.

The thrill of adventure hung in the night air, as I raced down the garden steps, passed the creature under the decking snuffling about and squeezed under the gate… back to the secret clearing and Athelstan materialised at once.

"A gentleman farmer needs a bit of help with his digging," was all the woody gatekeeper would say.

I followed Yulia and she spoke a curious rhyme, heard no doubt from Da,

"Sow four grains in a row,
One for the pigeon, one for the crow,
One to rot and one to grow."

She shushed me out of the tunnel and I found myself on the edge of a ploughed field. It looked very bare and bleak. I had no idea what century I was in until a man in a wig approached, leading a horse to which a strange wooden cart-like contraption had been harnessed.

Being an intelligent dog I guessed it was the 1700s. I watched as he climbed on the back of the cart and encouraged the horse to walk in a straight line, steering him from behind by means of reins and a long whip; the 'cart' was dragged, disturbing the earth and making a furrow or trench, and then seed was dropped in the ground at regular intervals.

This had to be better than the old method of 'broadcasting' which was merely walking and scattering seed on the surface of the field by hand, hoping for a good harvest. Hence Yulia's curious rhyme.

I heard a familiar voice and turned to see Yulia waving frantically at me from the entrance of the tunnel.

"Come back Rolo – we're in Berkshire. Wrong turning! We need to head east!"

I obediently scampered back in the hole, disappointed not to be able to so much as a sniff at this exciting 18th century field. We retraced our steps deep underground and took another branch in the tunnel and this time came out in Raynham, Norfolk on the estate of Lord Townshend. Same sort of time scale I reckoned.

Lord Townshend was a former diplomat who became a farmer, and he found the horse drawn seed drill of his contemporary in Berkshire to be wasteful and not quite living up to its promise to increase the arable farmer's crop by cutting down on wastage.

Lord Townshend was experimenting with growing other crops with different types of root systems so that they would take their goodness from varying depths of the soil, thereby removing the need to leave a field empty ('fallow') for a season, so he could really maximise the yield of his crop. He was also experimenting with draining the soil and adding manure and 'marl' (a type of fertiliser made from lime and clay) so he could really enrich the soil. The problem was that the roots of the crops such as barley and wheat were quite shallow and took their nourishment from the same depth, quite close to the surface. He thought about rotating these crops with clover which could be used as animal feed. Clover grew right on the surface spreading its spidery roots thinly, barely needing any soil to grow.

(Later, relaying this to Athelstan, I asked him if 'marl' was anything to do with the town of Marlborough. Ha! I had him there! The wise old gatekeeper didn't know the answer to that one! Local people think Marlborough means Merlin's Barrow but Athelstan snorted at that suggestion.)

When I found Lord Townshend standing in a field and scratching his head under his powdered wig, I went to work and dug a hole, like Athelstan had said. The reason I did that was because I could smell something quite exciting, like buried treasure, but in reality a long-forgotten smelly old animal bone. The man watched me with interest and when the flying clods of earth hit him on the head, he had a 'Eureka' moment much as Percy Shaw had.

"By Jove you've got it!" Townshend cried out loud to his bemused estate workers. "We need to dig deeper – if we plant turnips, that will rest the top soil for a season and also give us animal fodder through the winter without the need to leave the whole field fallow!"

This became known as the Norfolk Four Course Rotation method – turnips, oats or barley, clover and wheat were grown with successful precision improving the quality of British arable farming

117

forever. The farmer who introduced this nationally became 'Turnip' Townshend' and no one knows it's all down to the digging skills of a Jack Russell! Quick though, no time to bask in glory back to the 21st century and into my basket before I am missed, just stopping to puff and blow down the crack in the decking on my way back to the house. Just so you know, whatever you are, that I am watching you…

I squeezed my way through the trapdoor and jumped down onto the kitchen floor. Oh no! muddy paw prints! Luckily the under sink cupboard was full of cleaning cloths so I dragged one out with my teeth and stood on it, doing a little dance on the floor to wipe up the mud. Phew, that was close!

Dog blog #8 According to Rolo

The coast's clear…Here I am back at the keyboard.

I overheard the smiley lady asking the floppy haired boy if he'd been using her cleaning cloths to wipe his skateboard. She told him to use the ones in the garage. He denied it. Oops, I think I got him into trouble.

The smiley lady was told by the dogs home when she signed for me, that Jack Russells don't like rain… what a load of old tosh - it washes the wheat field track (known to local dog walkers as poo alley) clean and everything smells fresh out there.

I don't think the smiley lady minds the rain too much either — she's got a black plastic raincoat with luminous flashes that makes her look like a firewoman. We don't seem to meet any other dogs or their owners today though. The smiley lady said to me if we waited for it to stop raining I'd be crossing my little furry legs for a week!

We have a right little pantomime when we return from a wet walk… she carries me wrapped in a towel to the utility room, shuts herself in there with me and then attacks me with the towel and then a firm brushing.

When I am finally released from the 'wet' room, I wipe myself all-round the newly covered green and blue settees. The lady is not smiling and doesn't seem to like this action and keeps shutting the lounge doors to keep me out. Spoilsport, as now I can't sit on the back of the settee in the window to wait for the postman - my favourite viewing perch.

Haha, the smiley lady thought
she was going to sit and watch
Wimbledon tennis all afternoon on
the telly, but that doesn't look
too likely as it's raining in that
place too. She's changed all the
beds but can't dry the sheets —
silly lady; fancy doing the washing
on a rainy summer's day!

I met the other Nanny and Grandad
earlier this week (well that's what
the floppy haired boy calls them so
I will too). I was very good and
didn't wee up their curtains as
they had feared I might, nor did
I dig in their garden and Nanny
gave me an 'all butter shortbread'
biscuit and said I was a good boy.

I hope we will be going there on
a regular basis. I see the smiley
lady has put some dog biscuits in

a pot to take to Nanny's next time though - how disappointing. She spoils all my fun. I will call this nice lady 'Nanny Biscuits' from now on.

I have to confess I was a bit naughty early yesterday morning. Went for a long walk with the smiley lady and kept her in sight and came back every time she called me. She has bought a dog whistle, figuring the sound would carry further in a wheat field than the human voice.

She's right of course and the little booklet tells her that different sounds can encourage me to sit at a distance, come, stay, etc.If I'm not careful she'll have me rounding up sheep next! She's been training me to come when

called with the aid of a smear of
cheese triangle on a rubber chicken
leg (oh pleeeeeease! - She says
Waitrose don't do my favourite
soft cheese in tubes which is what
they used to train us with at Dogs
Trust).

Anyway I went along with it all…
and then got a bit overexcited
when we got back to the big field
at the end of the long walk and I
suddenly remembered the flat cats in
the garden down the alleyway and I
wanted to see if their eyes really
did reflect like the 'catseyes'
invention, so I took off, before the
lady had a chance to reattach the
lead at the top of the alley way
where she usually reclaims me.

In my defence I completely
ignored the flat cats (yes I know

they're not real and all about
their reflective eyes) and instead
explored every front garden and
gate in the cul-de-sac.

The lady was a comical sight
furiously whispering 'Rolo', not
wanting to use the new whistle as
it was only 7.30 on Sunday morning
and we were the only two up judging
by the firmly drawn curtains along
the street. I got a big telling off

The Secret Adventures of Rolo

and no reward biscuits and was shut in the kitchen on our return home; but we made up later.

We've had lots of long walks, the smiley lady and I -The trouble is she gets just as tired as I do and sometimes we both stretch out on the settee in the warm sunshine of the conservatory and have a secret zzzzzz in the afternoon if we can get away with it.

The only trouble with the conservatory is that big curious bumble bees come in through the open window. They make a very loud buzzing sound as they scan all the windows presumably looking for a way back out into the sweet smelling garden. They are lured indoors by the bright geraniums the smiley lady grows in pots just like

her grandmother did. I try to catch
the buzzy bees in my mouth.
The smiley lady gets hysterical and
opens the door and shushes them
out. She says her name means 'bee'
and we must never hurt them. She
says they would hurt me given half
the chance, though, and I'm not to
try to eat them.

Just now the postman came (enemy
number two second only to the
neighbour's cat) and he poked a
soft parcel through the letter box.
As the lady was dozing off I thought
I'd help him and managed to pull it
right through for the smiley lady.

I'm so clever. She was cross
though… I was only trying to help
her open it… There were only a few
tooth marks on it and the postman
still has all his fingers.

Hoping for an evening at the Cricket Club watching the floppy haired boy but the smiley lady keeps looking out the window and tutting... not sure the match will be on as it's still raining. Catch you later.

Dog blog #9 According to Rolo

I haven't had a chance to get on here for a couple of days so here goes...

The smiley lady found out something she started to suspect a week ago - I LOVE WATER! Today she took me to Hungerford Marshes and I had a lovely walk and paddled in the little ford, then wallowed in the thick black mud of the marshes and jumped in the canal to clean myself. I got a bit of a telling off as I can hear my name and the whistle but I'm just too busy and I know my fun is going to be curtailed when she calls. When it comes to water I just can't help myself. I am a champion doggy paddler. Poor lady has a mild coronary worrying whether I can get out again…

Later on, during the walk back through Hungerford Town, I really wanted to hook a duck from the canal (there were plenty and all were quacking at me), but she wouldn't let me off my lead so I went in anyway, swam in a circle and got lifted unceremoniously out. This, of course, washed the mud off but I honked a bit from the canal water, so I ended up plonked in the sink in the utility room when we got home. Washed, shampooed and then put outside to shake dry, then towel rubbed and brushed and dried in a rare moment of sunshine… Now I smell of damp dog but at least I'm clean!

Now laying on my blanket and licking my paws to make sure. The smiley lady won't let me go to sleep for some reason - she's afraid I won't go to bed in a couple of hours - but I'm dog tired. Besides, I'm sure Athelstan has another Very Important Errand for me.

Oh yes and at bed time last night I overheard the smiley lady and the floppy haired boy saying how funny it was that I didn't mind being shut in the kitchen anymore and how quickly I'd settled in. If only they knew what I was up to at night whilst they slept in their beds! 'Night all.

Chapter 9

Understory Adventure – Rolo and the Biscuit Tins

"Is there anything in particular you would like to find out about, Rolo?" asked Athelstan the next time we met. It seemed I could go anywhere at any time through the amazing time tunnel, as long as I had the pink ball to gain access to it through the base of the tree trunk. I thought for a moment and replied,

"I'd like to find out why people keep their biscuits in tins. It's very annoying as I can't get at the contents." This was prompted by Nanny Biscuits and the fancy tin she keeps my biscuits in.

Athelstan smiled his woody smile and said,

"Then you need to go to Reading to find out. Keep away from the canal, though." I wondered how Athelstan was so wise; he seemed to know about everything, even my swimming adventures!

I placed the pink ball at the foot of the tree and, whilst Yulia was lighting my way down the time tunnel, I asked her if she knew anything about the old English rhyme which predicted what sort of summer weather may lie ahead. I saw her tiny face smile in the lantern light and she said:

"Ash before oak and we shall have a soak. Oak before ash and we shall have a splash." She went on to enlighten me: if the ash tree comes into leaf in the spring before the oak tree we are in for a wet summer. If the oak tree comes to bud before the ash tree it will be mainly dry. Clearly the ash tree had won nature's race this year then! I like asking Yulia these nature questions as she has all this wonderful knowledge from Da, passed down as it should be.

This time I emerged in the middle of the built up town of Reading, but this was in olden times, way before the invention of the motor car. Round about the19th century I reckoned. A huge red brick factory with tall chimneys stood in front of me with the name Huntley and Palmer painted in big white letters. The heavenly smell of freshly baked biscuits filled the air. I watched a black horse pulling a carriage draw up to the front of the building and stop whilst parcels of biscuits were carried out by hand and carefully loaded onto the carriage.

The driver was thrust a piece of paper to sign and

could be heard muttering about not guaranteeing the safe delivery of the biscuits as the road between Reading and London was in a poor state of repair with many pot holes.

The biscuit factory foreman tutted and said that he had to sign the piece of paper or he couldn't take the biscuits. I wondered if that was where the expression 'taking the biscuit' came from. Must remember to ask Athelstan later; he seems to know everything. Eventually the driver signed the docket with the proffered quill and the stage coach clattered off over the cobbled streets, no doubt shaking its load to crumbs on the long journey by road up to the capital city.

I followed the foreman into the factory, drawn in by the delicious aroma which filled the busy workplace. They didn't smell like dog biscuits... Altogether sweeter and much more exciting. I sniffed around, hoovering the floor, hoping to find a crumb or two, but it was kept immaculately clean and swept.... no one seemed to take any notice of me. I heard the foreman talking to another man about the problems of transportation. It seemed these biscuits also travelled west from Reading to Bristol and Bath by waterway.

That seemed sensible – a far gentler mode of transport. However, they were saying that the problem with using this type of transportation was the length of time it took for the barge to be horse-drawn the length of the Kennet and Avon Canal and that the biscuits were often stale on arrival, even if they were still in one piece. There were also many locks and a number of flights of locks to navigate; all of which were very time consuming.

Between them, the men came up with the idea of packing the biscuits in a tin. This would keep the biscuits fresh and stop them being damaged in transit. All this talk of biscuits made me hungry. I wanted to taste a sample and saw a door marked 'store room' so I ducked in and managed to find a few broken biscuits on the floor.

Unobserved, I tucked in to these delicious and usually forbidden sweet treats. But ow my tooth hurt. I am sure the ring on the trapdoor under the sink was loosening it. I heard the male voices continue their discussion in the corridor and decided it would be best to stay hidden.

There was a bit of history on a poster mounted on the wall. The first biscuits were made by Joseph Huntley in 1822 near The Crown coaching inn on the busy London Road. He sold freshly baked individual biscuits to hungry coach travellers from a basket and then went into business with George Palmer, who bought the shop next door.

As the business grew, they had to find the means to transport the fresh baked biscuits further afield more efficiently.

Without realising it, the discussion I was listening to seemed to be about the origin of biscuit tins. They were talking about the design. The tins were to be large and square, handmade from tin plate by Joseph Huntley's youngest son, also named Joseph, in his ironmonger's shop opposite the bakery. He also had an idea to make shop-display tins with glass lids. Grocers could then sell biscuits from the big tin in the shop by weight and put them in paper bags when sold to individual customers.

I found out later from Athelstan, who knows all things, that when railways started to be used as a quicker means of transport for reaching customers quicker than by canal or road, the tins had to be re-shaped to have a long side, as these would fit better in Great Western Railways' goods carriages than the square tins.

Nanny Biscuits keeps my treats in a tin. I bet she'd be fascinated to learn all this information. Such a shame I can't tell her! Nor can I open the bloomin' tin and help myself when she is busy talking to the smiley lady and they are ignoring me.

Dog blog #10 According to Rolo

Whew, I had no idea my life could get any more exciting, and sorry I haven't had the chance to blog for a while!

At the weekend the lady had a visitor, an old friend, and she and this Scottish lady took me romping on the Downs at Pewsey Vale — wow, it was such good fun! There were hares to chase, wild flowers to sniff and rabbit holes to explore (although the lady kept grabbing my collar to stop me disappearing — not to worry, these were only ordinary holes and not magical tunnels of secret adventure! Not that she'd know about those of course).

Then they stopped for refreshment at The Barge at Honey Street, right on the canal, and I had the chance to watch some barges and remember my last adventure. Finally home to watch the Wimbledon Final. The people had a big roast dinner and I hoovered up the dining room carpet. They are such messy eaters.

Then the smiley lady's other son arrived home for a few days with a friend and they brought a house rabbit with them. I thought it was for me to look after and play with. I only know about this because I've overheard them talking about a little bunny called Onyx. I went out for a walk and it seems it got smuggled upstairs. I can smell it but I can't see it… I just have a feeling there's something going on beyond the stairgate.

The lady keeps quoting 'Finding Nemo' at me — 'friends not food' - and she is really nervous about us meeting up for some reason. Everyone is hysterically shutting the gate almost before they go through it. There is tension in da house. Oops they're coming…

Sorry about that… Back again…

The fields beyond the track along

our usual wheat field walk have turned blue. It's flax. It's an amazing sight even to a dog which should really be colour blind. You forget I'm special.

I'm making an extra effort to come when called but it is difficult when I'm following a scent and am I'm used to being so independent when out on my adventures. I polished off a tub of sour cream and chive dip which the floppy haired boy's brother (the one with the bunny) had casually left on the table.

I was very nearly sick but managed to just about hold it together. The previous night the boys gave me a half-eaten corn on the cob and I ate the husk and not just the yellow corn kernels, much to their amusement. The smiley lady stopped smiling when she knew what they'd done as she's quite strict with me (actually she doesn't know I polished off a piece of River Cottage recipe Banana Chocolate Cardamom Loaf when she wasn't looking). I'm such a greedy little dog with big puppy eyes.

Am exhausted and pretending to sleep but have an ear up as the lady is about to serve dinner – ever hopeful – During my 'clown eyes' moment of vision this afternoon, I saw horses. Big horses. Better get off the laptop now.

August: 'If St Bartholomew's (24 August) is clear, a prosperous autumn comes that year.'

Under the late summer sun the crops in the fields turn from deep green to golden brown. The farmer knows how long to leave the

The Secret Adventures of Rolo

ripening ears and when to harvest the crop before too much rain comes. He times it just right. The best sound at this time is the rustling of the wind in a ripe cornfield. Crouch down on the edge of one and listen to the shushing, almost like the sea.

When the corn is cut, many woodland creatures lose their homes; field mice, voles, rats and rabbits really suffer. Hills are carpeted purple and white with heather. Fruits appear on orchard trees; plums in particular attract wasps and butterflies. Keen eyed nature watchers can spy tiny pipistrelle bats at twilight, circling over-head, and if you are lucky you might find a hedgehog in your garden! See how many different types of butterflies you can see, particularly if you have a buddleia (butter-fly bush) in your garden.

141

Chapter 10

Understory Adventure – Rolo Meets the Wadworth Shire Horses

Summoned by Yulia and the owl in the usual way, I was positively skipping as I scrambled through the undergrowth to the secret oak tree. I'd caught up on all my daytime sleep and was in a really happy mood and up for adventure.

Athelstan is sending me on a local mission tonight… to see the Wadworth shire horses. He wanted me to give them a message before they start their annual fortnight's holiday out to pasture in Poulshott.

The message was simply to say well done and to enjoy the freedom of romping around in a field grazing and just being horses. But something was wrong - the secret tunnel would not reveal itself and Athelstan had already faded back into the bark. I'd forgotten the pink ball!

That was the key to opening the tunnel. 'Well what was I supposed to do now?' I said out loud, not really expecting a response. 'You'll have to fetch the orb' the answer was whispered in the trees.

There was nothing else for it…I had to go home and find it. Now where was the pesky thing? I couldn't remember where I'd last had it…of course…under the kitchen sink…I must have dropped it on my way through the trapdoor. Which reminds me, my tooth has become so wobbly with all the trapdoor pulling, I think I may lose it!

Ah here's the ball…no time to waste…back down the steps and under the gate and back through the forest and there was Yulia and her Da standing in the open tunnel with a look of annoyance on their faces.

"Sorry I forgot the orb," I mumbled by way of apology and I'm sure I heard Athelstan snort.

I immediately recognised the neighbouring town

of Devizes where the time tunnel led to this time.
I made my way to the stable at the back of the
Wadworth brewery. The horses have usually finished
their rounds by twelve noon and are then at rest for
the remainder of the day.

There are plenty of visitors waiting to see them, so I
wait for a family to finish lifting up their children to
pat the local four-footed heroes before I stand up on
my back legs and reach up within earshot of the big
horse called Monty. He leant down to greet me.

144

The Secret Adventures of Rolo

I gave him Athelstan's message and he nodded his wise head in acknowledgement. I moved out of the way as more fans were queuing up to say hello. I have seen these marvellous beasts at work. They walk majestically around the town, pulling heavily laden carts, never rushing, waiting patiently whilst full barrels are unloaded and empty ones collected.

I wouldn't like to get under their feet; they really are huge and truly 'heavy horses'. I feel quite humble in their presence. They do a very important job and are much loved. This was only a short visit and there was no point in hanging about. I would very much like to come back to Devizes for another adventure some time; I know there were once smugglers here!

I had seen the Wadworth shire horses before of course. Every time the smiley lady drives through the ancient market town of Devizes, she gets very excited when she sees the gentle four-legged giants pulling a dray, delivering famous Wadworth beer to the pubs within a two mile radius of the brewery. They hold up the traffic for a while, but the good people of Devizes don't mind. This is a tradition going back to 1875. The horses work either as a pair or singly and can pull up to two tons in weight.

They work fifty weeks of the year and very much earn their fortnight's holiday. The jollity always starts with a pint of 6X real ale at the Raven Inn and the horses are visited throughout their stay by well-wishers bearing gifts of apples and carrots, as there is a public footpath running through the field where they are turned out to graze.

Wait a minute: I didn't really need the tunnel or the pink ball for this mission! I could have easily passed on the message in broad daylight…well, if the smiley lady had taken me to Devizes that is - I couldn't exactly hop on a bus now could I? And I never know what her daily plans are, except that she usually takes me with her.

Dog blog #11 According to Rolo

The smiley lady's dad always calls

me Polo. When challenged as to why, he replies, "I knew your dog was named after a tube of sweets". Then he asks why the smiley lady calls me Polo. She replies, "I don't Dad, you do". They both find this terribly funny.

Yesterday we took him out in his wheelchair to a local park and I ran about a lot and didn't bark at the children penned in the 'no dogs allowed' playground, nor did I run on the croquet lawn. In fact, I was a very good boy. I will always think of him now as Granddad Polo.

Also saw Nanny Biscuits this week. She's the nice lady who gave me 'all butter shortbread fingers' the first time we met - I never forget details like this - but then the smiley lady gave her dog

The Secret Adventures of Rolo

biscuits locked in a tin, with strict instructions only to feed me one (well, two) at a time. - Now we know they are in a tin to stop them going soft. However, when the smiley lady wasn't looking, Nanny Biscuits poured gravy on my doggy biscuit dinner…yum yum yum. I love her.

The big boy has gone back to London. This is a shame because he let me lick out yoghurt pots, polish off dips and eat crisps. He took the mysterious rabbit with him (yes, I know you all think I didn't know there was a rabbit living upstairs…of course I did, even though I never got to see it!)

Shame, we could have been such good friends. Perhaps posed for a cute calendar photo?

Today it's been pouring with rain
and the smiley lady had some
friends visiting from overseas.
They drove up so quietly outside
the house I didn't even bark.The
children were very energetic and we
went to the fun forest beyond the
garden, but I was careful not to
lead them near Athelstan's gateway.

It was still pouring with rain
and I went in every puddle and
so did they, as they don't see
much rain living most of the year
in a very hot climate. Lots of

149

wild raspberries to eat — didn't
see what all the fuss was about
— funny little bobbly red fruit,
don't really float my boat. Home
for drying and brushing and a big
sleep… (yawn)… after I've finished
blogging of course…

Dog blog #12 According to Rolo

Quick update whilst no-one's
looking…

Ok, I lied when I said I didn't
like raspberries. This morning
the sun came out and we went back
to the woods and the smiley lady
picked a whole load for jam making.
I tried one and decided I liked
them after all and helped myself to
the ones I could reach, plucking
them right off the low lying bushes
- just my height.

The smiley lady was amazed. I had to lend her a poo bag as she forgot to bring a pot to collect the red berries in - an unused one I hasten to add.

There is a delicious aroma in the kitchen… Warm jam cooling in glistening glass jars. Tired out and ready for a little power nap… it's hard work being me sometimes.

The floppy haired boy flipped me over and rubbed my tummy like he usually does. I love him. He noticed that my wobbly tooth had come out. "Not much we can do about that," said the smiley lady. "Wonder how Rolo managed to lose it?"

Chapter 11

Understory adventure - Thomas Wolsey… Rolo drops a clanger

"Brave little pup, I have another local historic event for you to witness," said Athelstan from his usual barky wrap around the oak tree.

The tiny woodland folk already had their instructions and when they told me we were going to the redundant church in the High Street called St Peters, I wondered at the necessity of using the time tunnel as this was only a short walk downhill from home.

"Silly Paddy Paws!" exclaimed Yulia, "you need to go back to 1498 and I doubt the landscape of the town now resembles anything like what you are going to see. For a start, there wasn't a road running either side of the church making it into an island!"

I felt rather foolish and decided best not to speak at

all to save further embarrassment.

Coming out from the time tunnel at the west end
of the High Street I saw exactly what Yulia meant.
The church stood proudly in a field and at the other
end I saw St Mary's of the cat-in-the-fire drama,
although that wouldn't even happen for another 150
years or so.

As I approached the rather grand Norman church
with fine square tower enclosed within the width
of the famously wide High Street (in the 15th
century just a wide cart track), I realised that a
ceremony of some importance was about to happen.
I mingled with the townsfolk, away from the solemn
procession of dignitaries and stood just inside the
porch door to see what was going on. It turned
out to be the ordination of a priest. 'Not terribly
exciting,' I thought to myself.

Then I did a double take as the young priest who
was to be ordained approached, following the bishop
in his tall mitre carrying the traditional crook. I

recognised the man from likenesses in history books and dotted around the church in modern times; this was Thomas Wolsey. Athelstan had told me about the butcher's son who would go on to negotiate the tricky 'Field of the Cloth of Gold' meeting between King Henry Vlll and Francis l of France some 20 years later. He had risen high in the King's favour by then, playing off allegiances with the Pope in Rome with the all-powerful France and Spain, changing sides to suit his advantage.

Cardinal Wolsey famously engineered the break with the church in Rome over Henry Vlll's divorce from Catherine of Aragon, so that the king was free to pursue and eventually marry Ann Boleyn. This created the Church of England split from the church in Rome, although Wolsey failed in his promise to secure an annulment to the marriage from the Pope.

Because of this failing, Ann Boleyn ultimately engineered the greedy cardinal's downfall and arrest in 1529 as she saw him as being too power hungry for his own personal gain rather than acting out of loyalty to the Crown (or more precisely, the would-be queen). All this preceded the Queen's own execution in 1536.

But that was in his future. Young Thomas Wolsey was about to be ordained a priest. There is a commotion on the steps. The crowd are jostling to follow the procession into the nave of the church.

"Out," shouted a thickset man brandishing a pike. He resembled a bookend as he was identical to his partner; same height and stature and unsmiling face. They could have been ancestors of the guardsmen on the common during the Civil War!

"No dogs allowed in a holy building." The crowd parted to let me exit the building with some dignity. I didn't think I could communicate with this ignorant peasant and anyway I doubted he would listen. I realised that there was no way I was going to get passed these two lumps and so I sat down in the churchyard and gathered my feet in. I had to rethink my strategy.

Opposite the churchyard and along the track a
little was a hostelry called The Star. I ducked inside
unchallenged and overheard two serving girls
complaining that they didn't want to work today
as it was their day off, but the landlord said it was
going to be very busy in the inn after the ordination
ceremony.

To avoid being seen by these ladies, who seemed
to be doing something to the barrels of ale with
a pitcher of water, I snuck under the bar and
immediately spied a small door, and being naturally
curious, I pushed it open and went in. I almost fell
headlong down a steep ladder…and there I was in
the cellar. No idea what might be down there other
than barrels of beer and butts of wine, but having
nothing better to do I scampered in the dark and
found a narrow passageway.

Of course, as you knew I would, I pressed on. I
edged my way through the darkness, without the
benefit of Yulia and her Da's pin pricks of light to
help me find my way. I sniffed along the very cold

and damp smelly stone walls of the passageway which seemed to go on forever, and then I hit a dead end. What now? Here I was underneath The Star…or was I? I seemed to have travelled a fair distance underground. Maybe this would come up somewhere else.

I looked around in the dark and saw the vague outline of a square of light above me…a trapdoor! But where was I? I pushed it open with my head and stuck my paws through and heaved myself up through the hole. I could hear voices, chanting in Latin, and realised I must be somewhere in the church! I'd managed to get in to see the Ordination of Wolsey after all! The trapdoor had come out in a very narrow space and here I was in the base of the church tower, just inside the porch where the heavies were standing on the other side of the wooden door. How lucky was that! I bounded up the stone spiral staircase thinking I would get a better view of the proceedings from above.

Something nudged me: Sturdy rope. Now, if I could

get hold of it in my teeth I could manoeuvre myself to a better viewing position. Unfortunately for me, it was not an ordinary rope hanging there. It was attached to an enormous bronze bell, and just at the relevant part of the solemn ceremony taking place in the nave of the church below, a very loud clanging rang out, causing the whole congregation to wonder if it was in fact a sign from the Almighty Himself.

The magnificent bell was not scheduled to be rung until after the ceremony had finished. The bishop paused mid-sentence, but was assured in a whisper by a member of the clergy that it was an over-zealous bell ringer who would be severely

The Secret Adventures of Rolo

dealt with afterwards for disturbing the solemn proceedings. Oops! Better get out of there before I was discovered 'red pawed'; it didn't seem that exciting an event anyway.

I knew I had dropped a clanger and wondered who would get into trouble instead of me. I also thought it best not to hang around so I let go of the rope, causing the bell to toll even more frantically. I exited the church the same way, back through the trapdoor, along the damp passageway and back into the cellar, up the steep steps and out through the Inn, much to the amusement of the serving girls who were still busily watering down the ale.

Outside The Star in the empty street, I saw a man being set upon by two robbers; presumably they were opportunists who saw rich pickings at a big gathering of townsfolk for a church event. I barked at them and snapped around their ankles and, although they tried to kick me away, I didn't give up. Eventually they fled, and their victim was very grateful, clutching his purse and patting me. He gave me a morsel of bread from his pack by way of reward and he poured wine from a skin into the palm of his hand so I could have a drink. I couldn't communicate with him, but I wagged my tail.

He looked nervously around. I could see the escaping robbers who probably thought they'd got away with their haul. Bold as brass they had squatted down under a tall tree and they were emptying out the loot on the ground, presumably to share it before going their separate ways. The man I had just saved was brushing himself down and took his leave of the scene.

He didn't seem to want to do anything about the robbers; thanks to me, nothing of his had been stolen. Rather selfish I thought. He disappeared in the direction of the town. What to do now? I couldn't let them escape justice. How could I restrain these robbers? They were drinking something from a skin bottle, passing it between them and staggering about. No doubt celebrating their good fortune. That might work to my advantage.

I ducked inside the back entrance of The Star and saw a coil of rope lying in the yard. I picked it up in my teeth and carried it to the base of the tree. They didn't even notice me as their greedy eyes took in the value of their haul. I used the element of surprise to confound the men as they sat leaning their backs against the tree, and quick as anything I ran round and round, barking as fiercely as I could, having flung the rope coil diagonally over my shoulder; I managed in this way to secure them to the tree.

I think they may have had too much to drink, as they certainly seemed incapable of putting up a fight. I could see a silver goblet and some jewellery lying scattered on the ground.

The ceremony was still going on inside St Peters and, as there was no one else likely to enter the church building at this time, I thought I could perhaps draw the attention of the guards and alert them to this crime scene, in the absence of any kind of police force as we were only at the end of the 15th century.

"You again!" roared one of the guards as I jumped up and niftily dodged his hefty boot. He kicked the wall instead and cursed. Not good for a church guard, I thought. I somehow had to get them to follow me. I jumped up at the other one and plucked his coin purse from his belt in my teeth and made off with it. That had the desired effect!

"Why you little...come back here!" and I fled the scene with the purse in my mouth, drawing them towards the two befuddled robbers I had left roped together round the tree.

"Heavens preserve us, what have we got here?" said the one whose purse I had pinched; his item now forgotten.

"Oh no, Reynold, we can't be having no crime on our patch. We're supposed to be on guard duty round here. We're up for promotion to the King's Guard if all goes well on our watch today!"
"Well what do we do now? We won't get promoted if this gets out, and worse, we might be blamed!" said

162

Percy.

"Well, there's only one thing for it…we have to dig… get rid of the hoard."

"We can always come back for it later" said Reynold, slyly. "Remember where we're burying it."

I gave a little yelp. I could help with the digging I knew full well, and by the glint in these oafs' eyes that's exactly what they were thinking. I backed away, barking and dropped the guard's purse. Not very heroic, but there was nothing I could do about these stolen jewels other than flee the scene.

I certainly didn't intend to become an accessory to helping them hide the loot for their own ill-gotten gain! I ran for it, as fast as my short furry legs would carry me, all the way back to the time tunnel entrance and was too breathless to tell Yulia what had happened. As I glanced back over my shoulder, I saw the two men set to work with shovels, no doubt borrowed from The Star, digging away at the mud, right next to the spot where the robbers slumped, snoring their heads off, tied together back to back and probably dreaming of how they would spend their loot.

Must remember to wipe my feet as I go back through the trapdoor this time.

Dog blog #13 According to Rolo

It's been difficult to get on here lately with the floppy haired boy not being at school for the holidays… I have to wait till he's gone out on his skateboard.

This week I discovered I am a real foodie dog. Having recently developed a taste for raspberries, I also find I love olives, mozzarella cheese and sun-dried tomatoes and any other fine foods left on the coffee table at nose

The Secret Adventures of Rolo

height. Everyone went out into the garage to admire the newly made grind-box (something to do with the boy with the floppy hair's summer DT project) and I seized the main chance.

Most affronted to be caught in the act and lifted unceremoniously off the coffee table just as I was getting to slurp up the olive oil... 'A dog of good taste but not very good manners,' the smiley lady said crossly.

Lovely weather at last — perfect for romping the Downs and we went to Fyfield and found lots of big ancient stones lying about in fields which made the smiley lady very happy. They were called grey wethers because from a distance they apparently resemble sheep

(also called wethers). I suppose
they do. Just the right height for
weeing on as far as I'm concerned.
Another day we went to West Woods
and found many muddy puddles
despite 4 days of drying sunshine.
So, another bath in the sink
awaited me at home as my original
base colour is white.

One summer evening the smiley lady
took me to Potterne and I watched
her jolly friend muck out some
horses and discovered that I quite
like the taste of horse poo much
to my not-so-smiley lady's horror.
Well it's just recycled grass isn't
it?

We had a marvellous walk from
Potterne Cricket Club all around
the edge of a wheat field and past
One Tree Hill. New territory to

explore, ending up in a pub in Urchfont, but alas neither beer nor chicken curry came my way, just for the ladies…grrrrr.

I know the shire horses like to drink beer and I would have liked to taste it. Instead I sat quietly under the table in the evening sunshine and was much admired by the eaters and drinkers in the pub garden.

The smiley lady hired a big noisy machine and spent the next day cleaning the carpets so I was banished from the house. Every time I came in I had to stop on the doorstep to have my paws wiped for the umpteenth time. Oh the indignity of it all. Made the mistake of weeing on the kitchen tiles this morning.I knew straight away I shouldn't have done it and hoped it would quickly evaporate, but alas, no, it was discovered and I was in the dog house for a while. I wanted to point out that at least it wasn't on the newly shampooed carpets, but no one was listening.

Right. Time for a little nap and then hopefully off for more adventure.

Dog blog #14 According to Rolo

The coast's clear…here I am again with an update…

I may be a very intelligent Jack Russell but I am a tad confused. the lady calls me Rolo, Granddad calls me Polo and the boy with floppy hair now calls me YOLO (only teenagers will know what that means

— Athelstan translated for me:
You Only Live Once) So basically
I answer to anything 'olo and
definitely not Ronnie which is the
name I came with along with the
yellow lead, tag and harness from
Dog's Trust, which seems a lifetime
ago.

Now to confess to you a prickly
problem I have… I seem to be a bit
of a hedgehog magnet. Not sure what
this is all about but I've found 5
in the last month and none of them
want to play.
They curl up tightly in a ball
and I keep jabbing them with my
nose and whining but they won't DO
anything! It's got to the point now
(no pun intended) where I am not
allowed off the lead at night on the
field because I ALWAYS find one. Good
to know hedgehogs are alive and

well and living in Wiltshire!

An unusual day yesterday for a small dog. Dropped off the car in a garage in the big noisy town of Swindon as it had to be serviced, which meant transferring my pop up travelling box to a 'courtesy car' (confusingly also called a Polo) and then a couple of hours spent at Barbury Castle ancient hill fort waiting for the smiley lady's car to be ready for collection.

We enjoyed a blustery walk around the top of the chalk ridges (it always blows a gale up there). Surprised to see so many wild flowers out; blue harebells, red campion, clover, ragged robin, yellow bird's foot trefoil and bright blue tall scabious — so late this year.

We sat on the top of the ridge and watched the storm clouds gathering... and, yes, you've guessed it, the heavens opened and it poured! I raced the not-so-smiley lady back to the borrowed car. Back at the VW garage, drying out, I was a very good boy sitting on the smiley lady's lap in the waiting area of the showroom whilst she drank coffee and shared a biscuit and everyone admired me.

She did laugh out loud at the advertisement for VW products in which every 6th sentence invited you to 'help yourself to tea and coffee and relax' and at the bottom of the frame it said 'terms and conditions apply'. She found that hilariously funny for some reason. I don't really get it.

Today the smiley lady made apple and onion chutney…the smell has brought the wasps in…I'm trying to catch one in my mouth to see what the buzzing feels like…she is going crazy trying to stop me.

I have a sneaky suspicion I'm home alone tonight as she's just taken me for a long walk…she and the floppy haired boy are off to dinner at a house with CATS.

Oh I wish they would take me… ah well, perhaps I can persuade a hedgehog to come indoors and play. I could hide it under the sink until they've gone out. At least I will be able to get on the laptop…

The next night before bed time:

The Secret Adventures of Rolo

DISASTER!!!! I've discovered what
was lurking beneath the decking in
the garden. It was a big old toad,
and when it stopped raining it came
out to catch some insects brought
out by the rain. I wanted to play
with it and pawed it a bit and then
it released some horrid tasting
poison from a sac near its mouth as
a means of defence.

Obviously the silly thing didn't
know I only wanted to play. Clearly
old toady didn't. Anyway this
stuff was evil and I'd swallowed
some and was literally frothing
at the mouth. The smiley lady was
hysterical and waving a torch; the
floppy haired boy was sent down the
garden to put me on my lead, remove
whatever I was playing with and
bring me indoors at once. I drank

The Secret Adventures of Rolo

a huge bowl of water and went to
bed feeling very sorry for myself.
The normally smiley lady had a
sleepless night worrying that I'd
been poisoned. Athelstan didn't
send for me. I dreamt of bonnets
and my sleep was troubled;I didn't
feel well at all.

The smiley lady came downstairs
very early the next morning worried
that when she let me out in the
garden I would resume playing with
the participant of the previous
night's shenanigans.

She's not very good at dealing with
stuff so she walked down the garden
not really looking for the crime
scene, carrying a large flower pot
to put over the corpse for someone
else to deal with later, but it had
gone! So I had been wrongly accused

of murdering the toad, and actually hadn't killed anything after all. There was no evidence m'lud!

A few days later I could smell the thing under the decking again and the floppy haired boy and his mates lifted a paving slab and saw the damaged but very much alive toad back in its usual hiding place.

I watched all this from the window as they wouldn't let me near it. So, just to let you know, my name is cleared: I AM NOT A TOAD KILLER! ROLO IS INNOCENT!

Chapter 12

Rolo's Understory – Haxey Hood…Rolo Retrieves the Bonnet

Da's words of country wisdom for September: "if you see a sheep graze with his head to the wind expect fine weather; if his tail is to the wind rain will come."

Nature's pallet turns to autumn shades; the merest tint of yellows, browns, ochre in the sycamore, beech, elm and birch trees.

Crab apples in crop and berries appear on hawthorn, elder, mountain ash, yew and dogwood. There is a chill in the air and fingers of mist linger in the valley until after sunrise.

Hips and haws in vivid red brighten the hedgerows. The fields are harvested and will be ploughed ready for the next crop.

Gulls and rooks scavenge the empty fields. Maple trees drop their fruit and leaves are tinged with orange and the ash loses its tiny keys and turns yellow.

The oak drops acorns and leaves turn brown.

The long arms of the beech tree are full of tawny leaves. Cones are now appearing on all cedar, pine, larch and spruce trees. Wasps are drawn to ivy flowers and all manner of fruit is being harvested.

Lapwings, linnets, greenfinches, hedge sparrows and tits are in abundance and many birds gather to migrate and others, including the redwing, will arrive. 'Fairy Rings' of mushrooms appear in fields and fungi of all shapes, sizes and colours can be spotted in the woods. See what you can find and draw or photograph, but don't touch! Some are highly poisonous.

"What has Athelstan got in store for me this time Yulia?" but the tiny woodland creature had already ducked back down the tunnel in search of warmth. "Too cold for man or beast," Da muttered as he turned on his heel and went underground.

Brrrrrrr it's cold. Early January I'd say looking at the frozen ground and the bare trees, and no idea where I am except that it is very rural and very flat. What on earth was I doing in this wasteland? I heard a shout; a few raised voices and then a handful of men, muddy from top to toe, romped towards me, staggering and tripping over furrows and ditches, and they appeared to be chasing something that was blowing over the fields. This looked to be a good game – I love chasing!

Without waiting for an invitation, I joined in. They were laughing because anytime any of them got close enough to put a hand to the object, a gust of wind would pick it up and carry it off, just out of reach. And so the game continued.

The object they were chasing looked to me like a lady's hat with long ties which were acting like the tail of a kite causing it to swoop up in the air. It was nearly within my grasp and with a flying leap I got about a foot off the ground and snatched the ribbons of the runaway bonnet in my teeth.

The men fell about laughing in the mud and encouraged me to drop the hat. I'm good at 'fetch' but not so good at 'drop' as you may know. So then they had to chase me, and the bonnet, back through the mud, through the ditches and over the fields until we came upon a lovely bare-headed lady sat astride a beautiful chestnut mare.

She had one hand on the reins and the other hand over her mouth and she was giggling. She was beautiful and I was star struck. I dropped the bonnet and the muddiest of the men swooped upon it, brushed it down his dirty clothes and handed it up to the lady with an exaggerated bow.

Bloomin' cheek; the lady would think he had captured the runaway hat, not me! Nothing I could do about it as I couldn't communicate with any of these people. Anyway, time to scamper back to Wiltshire through the time tunnel before it was morning and I would be missed. No idea what that adventure was all about.

Dog blog #15 According to Rolo

I'm using the smiley lady's laptop today, bear with me, the keyboard layout is a bit different...

Well, here I am in a different part of Wiltshire, having a little 'writing retreat' with the smiley lady in someone else's house. She writes a bit in the mornings and then we have lovely long doggy walks and then more writing (I sleep on her feet) and then to the pub for a drink in the evening (they welcome dogs round here!).

Today we drove to Cirencester Park; then a lovely romp up the long driveway and lots of posh dogs to sniff and chat to. We weren't allowed as far as the Polo Club… shame as I'd like to have seen a royal pukka chukka or two. Funny thing about the church tower at Cirencester, the further you walk away from it up the path, the taller the tower looks. The lady couldn't figure it out at all, but I think it's because the path inclines slightly so you see more of the tower the further away you walk. But what do I know? I'm just a Jack Russell making a scientific observation.

Anyway I jumped in a deep muddy puddle and came out with black boots so it was home for a bath in a washing up bowl. Oh the indignity of being bathed outside! But I'm now gleaming and spick and span. Off to the pub methinks.

By the way it's stuffed marrow for dinner…not for me thank goodness! People round here keep leaving marrows in a 'help yourself' basket placed in front of the village signpost. I wonder why? Don't people like them? Judging by what went in the bin I don't think the smiley lady was too keen on marrow either!

Dog blog #16...According to Rolo

Today I realised that the smiley lady also writes a blog, as I saw it left open on her laptop - she must do that when I'm sleeping - so I've copied and pasted one of hers so you can see what we got up to last weekend:

'You can't beat a glorious September weekend in the market town of Ludlow in Shropshire, especially when the Food Festival is on.

Sampling small tasters as we went, we followed a route mapped out on a helpful leaflet directing us on foot around the town to many stalls

selling local produce. We also
tried five famous Ludlow sausages
and voted marks out of ten for best
flavour, texture and appearance
on the famous 'Sausage Trail.'
My particular favourite was the
Gloucester Old Spot sausage served
at the Ludlow Food Centre.
Rolo managed to sample a few more

sausages by hanging round the
food stalls, doing his meerkat
impression, to which he has now
perfected Puss - from Shrek - eyes.
Needless to say we are now BOTH on
a strict diet!'

Not bad smiley lady, but I think my
writing style is better.

Chapter 13

Understory Adventure – Rolo flees Pompeii

Athelstan wants to send me further back in time than I have ever been. I wonder if this is going to take more than a night, but he just smiled and waved me off in the direction of the time tunnel where the two tiny lantern bearers were waiting.

This time we took a completely different direction once we had gone underground and I wondered how Yulia always seemed to know which path to choose to take us to the right time and place. It was all beyond me and she didn't seem in the mood to explain. In fact, the pair of them couldn't wait to be shot of me. I felt a sense of foreboding.

They told me we were in Italy, a place near what is modern day Naples. But way back in time. I was going to admire some artwork. When pressed, all Yulia would say to me regarding the timescale was that it was 79AD and I was in a pre-Roman flourishing city port and that something monumental was about to happen and I had better remember where the entrance to the tunnel was if I wanted to find myself back in my basket before morning. They tucked themselves back into the entrance and shooshed me outside and off on my adventure.

I stepped, blinking, into very warm sunshine. The air smelt of bay trees and I could see purple and white wisteria in full bloom, climbing all over some very elegant buildings. This was southern Italy; Pompeii to be exact. I found myself in front of an impressive villa opposite the Forum Baths, which was guarded by a very fierce type of dog known as a Molossi, a kind of forerunner of the Mastiff family.

He wasn't friendly at all in his welcome and he barked a warning; he was guarding and protecting the contents of the villa for his owner whom he referred to rather strangely as The Tragic Poet. Now I have no idea why this poet was tragic or even sad, but the whole place seemed full of doom and gloom and this dog seemed in no mood to tell me why. Luckily he was on the inside of the wall which surrounded the villa and I tried to reason with him, not least to stop his incessant barking. I couldn't hear myself think!

"Look here, my name is Rolo, I've come a long way on a fact-finding mission, sent by Athelstan." I spoke with more confidence than I felt.

The big dog was still slavering around his mean jaws but at least he stopped the racket for a moment to weigh me up and listen. He knew of Athelstan and gruffly woofed that his name was Brutus and he was a very important dog, not least because his likeness had been made into a mosaic in the vestibule of the villa. Would I like to admire it?

Well, that was a bit friendlier. It seemed rude not to take him up on the offer. I relaxed a bit. He opened the gate with his great hairy paw and I went in cautiously, avoiding eye contact with the imposing guard dog and politely sniffing his face to show he was the boss. I kept my tail wag low and he did the

The Secret Adventures of Rolo

same. We were eyeing each other up. I followed him, but not too closely, and we approached a covered hallway where he explained the private quarters of the house were situated.

I looked down at the floor and he stood four square waiting for some reaction. The mosaic we were standing on was very impressive indeed, striking in its black and white checkerboard pattern. The centrepiece did indeed seem to be a portrait of Brutus in all his vicious likeness, even down to the snarling teeth, although in the picture the ferocious dog was chained to a stake.

CAVE CANEM

188

The Secret Adventures of Rolo

The words 'Cave Canem' were inscribed underneath his huge paws, and when I queried this, Brutus translated from the Latin 'Beware of the Dog'. Well I never! He told me that his people were away from the area; he was just about to invite me to have a drink of water when our polite conversation was interrupted by a terribly loud rumbling, which seemed to come from the east of Pompeii itself.

Brutus sniffed the air in alarm and then started howling. This howl was taken up by other animals in the area and made a mournful din, far more unnerving than the fierce barking that had greeted my arrival in this unhappy place.

He paused for breath and explained to me that this was a barking chain acting as a system of warning; it would appear that the volcano Mount Vesuvius was about to blow her top. I saw something white fluttering through the air and thought at first it was snowing. It couldn't be though because it was so warm. Suddenly and unnaturally warm.

"Volcanic ash," hissed Brutus. "Look, little dog, I don't know where you've come from, but if I were you I would get out of here as quickly as you possibly can."

I didn't need telling twice. The air was now thick with swirling ash and a terrific heat came upon us, and a terrifying roar…

"Be quick that's molten lava; nothing can stand in its path," the dog warned, and I was gone. I skittered my back legs on the cobbles in my hurry to get back down the tunnel.

"Quick, Yulia and Da; we have no time to lose… We have to get away from this place and time…we're about to be engulfed by a volcanic eruption!"

I was rather surprised to see Athelstan's usually featureless face look somewhat relieved when we finally emerged panting from the time tunnel. I told him how I had nearly got caught up in the tragedy that was Pompeii, and he said:

"Well, let's face it little pup, you do like an adventure. You are nothing if not brave!" and more sombrely he added, "200,000 inhabitants of the city were killed as they went about their daily business that day…they would literally not have seen it coming.

The city was lost for many centuries, but when excavated in the nineteenth century, the remains of the people were found to be perfectly preserved in the ash and so their likenesses could be recreated by pouring plaster into moulds. Even the food they were eating and everyday objects from their homes."

'How eerie,' I thought and wondered privately whether Brutus's remains had been found. Athelstan turned then to the small folk:

"Thank you both for seeing him safely home." They nodded and made their way back among the tree roots to their understory home. I plodded wearily to mine, just as dawn was breaking.

Da's country wisdom for October : 'If ducks do slide at Hallowtide at Christmas they will swim; if ducks do swim at Hallowtide at Christmas they will slide.' (Hallowtide is 31 October, All Hallows, from where we get the name Halloween..)

Nature tops up her colour chart. Oaks are now a deeper bronze, elms are splashed with pale gold, beeches turn from copper to orange, and the birch is crowned with new gold, and sycamore, red.

Berries and fruits are abundant. Look out for shiny conkers. Keen-eyed nature spotters may be lucky to see a flash of blue and orange as hungry kingfishers dart along a stream looking for fish. Squirrels abound, feasting on beech masts, acorns and hazelnuts and wood-mice and birds demolish berries.

Solitary robins puff out their breasts and stand strong on splayed wiry legs and sing their little hearts out. They are territorial birds, and their song is by far the sweetest. If it's mild you might still see butterflies

hanging around in late sunshine; they may
venture indoors through an open window to
escape the onset of winter. Snakes and
lizards hibernate. With a new moon in the
sky, owls come out to hunt: brown owls,
barn owls, white owls and little owls. A rare
and wonderful sight. Lucky if you see one.

Most of the swallows and house martins
will leave for sunnier climes. A few wild geese
and ducks will arrive. An internal migration
occurs and you may see gatherings of
linnets, chaffinches, pipits and other

small birds. In the hedgerows young male
blackbirds squabble over borders of winter
quarters. Magpies, buzzards and red kites
can be seen, scouting around for food.

Dog blog #17 According to Rolo

Something's happening in the house…
At the end of October I saw the
lady get a suitcase out. Uh oh, I
thought. The floppy haired boy had
gone away for half term. Where on
earth was the smiley lady going,
and more importantly what was going
to happen to me? I knew she would
never put me in Kennels because she
promised me that.

She knew my history; I suffered
great trauma when I was pre-loved
and actually damaged my nose on the
wire of the pen at Dog's Trust due
to great stress, so I assumed I
was either going with her or that
someone was coming to look after
me. I warned Athelstan that this
dog may not be reporting for action
for a while. He said:

"Don't worry little pup — you've earned a holiday, go off and enjoy yourself and beware of sea monsters!" I shrugged and bounded home.

Sure enough the next day I got bundled into the car and sat very quietly for about two and a half hours, never once piping up from my back seat pop up tent with the dreaded words 'Are we there yet?', even though I thought it. Eventually we WERE there.

And this was a whole new adventure. Arriving in the late afternoon, we immediately set out across Thurlestone Golf Course following footpaths to Bantham. Clearly the grown-ups needed liquid refreshment after all that driving, but I was

way too excited with the wind under
my tail, jumping over the hillocks
of thrift on top of the cliffs,
finding rabbit holes and trying hard
to behave and not to go 'too close
to the edge'.

Highlight of this particular walk
was seeing the sea for the first
time — wow was it scary!
I ran at it and it roared and came
towards me and I barked at it and
it went back again. I spent an
hour doing this and I wouldn't let
it get the better of me. I wasn't
really scared but started to lose

The Secret Adventures of Rolo

my woof.

Then I had a fight with some seaweed. It was sticking out of the sand and I pulled and pulled and the sea roared at me and came towards me again then it went back and I pulled at the seaweed again but I couldn't budge it. What a great game! The smiley lady was laughing so much she bent over double; I don't know what she found so funny.

That was all sooooo exciting and there were lots of new friends to be made on the beach and then I found myself actually in the sea and jumping the waves and paddling about with a lurcher puppy and a collie.

Suddenly I turned into a salty

197

seadog! I had been warned not to drink the seawater, but it just looked like any big, albeit moving, puddle to me. Euuukkkk! I won't be in a hurry to do that again! The grown-ups had forgotten that the clocks going back made it dark, and it seemed later that it actually was. To cut a dog blog short, it was only 5.30 and the pub (The Sloop) didn't open till 6.30 so the smiley lady didn't get the fish pie she'd been looking forward to all day!

I slept really well and awoke early, ready for another seaside adventure. How did Athelstan know I was going to the seaside, I wondered?

This time we walked in the opposite direction, across South Milton

Sands to Hope Cove. A lovely uppy downy walk which left the grown-ups trying out all the benches someone had thoughtfully left strategically placed all along the cliff path for people out of breath. It was very very windy and my ears kept blowing inside out. Lucky really being small, I am close to the ground and get a bit of wind resistance being sheltered by bushes and suchlike. I wasn't allowed on the beach much today — well not in the sea anyway.

The sea was splashing up over the harbour walls at dear little Hope Cove, and I was ever so good in the Hope and Anchor pub whilst the grown-ups indulged in massive fish and chips for their late lunch. There were lots of other dogs sat quietly under the tables. We all stared and each other in sympathy.

A very long uphill walk home with the wind at our backs and then the heavens opened and we all got soaked. None of us cared though and after a good rub down with a dry towel, and with a full tummy, I'm curled up in my basket in front of the telly.

It's Halloween and there are a whole load of pumpkins in the old red phone box in the village. No idea what that's all about! It's usually a village second hand book exchange.

No doubt more adventures tomorrow — hope it's a bit drier under paw! I'm managing to type this whilst they're tidying up the kitchen before bed.

Dog blog #18 According to Rolo

I couldn't wait to get back out there in the seaside action this morning — it's just way too exciting here with so many other dogs, either on holiday like me or living here. Today we walked the steep road way to Bantham for lunch at what the smiley lady called 'the goldmine pub', otherwise known as The Sloop Inn.

The smiley lady had the smile wiped off her face though because their legendary fish pie was not available — although chef promised it would be back on the menu for Friday (fresh fish being steamed as we woof).

I sat under the table whilst they tucked into Lemon Sole with sweet potato and salad. Other grown-ups were feeding their dogs with chips but not mine… (sad face). It's a big pub and every table had a dog tucked underneath it: all shapes and sizes, from Yorkshire terriers to husky dogs and everything in between. It seems grown-ups don't go into a pub in Devon unless they have a dog. Not one of us made a sound. Not even a little whimper. There were no fights — it's as if we all followed the unwritten 'well-behaved doggy code' of sitting quietly under the table — we dogs know it's far better than the alternative of being left at home!

And then there was the promised romp on the beach afterwards. A surfing lesson was underway so I went to have a look. Another Jack

The Secret Adventures of Rolo

Russell ran off to chase rabbits in the sand dunes and my grown-ups asked me to assist her owner in finding her, which I did; silly girl. On the steep walk home over the coast path we were pelted with little balls of ice — how it did sting!

I've got a little scratch on my face. The smiley lady is not sure if I got it when I jumped up at a barbed wire fence to take a better look at a kite surfer below on the beach, or whether it was from one of the local dogs I was running the length of the beach with. Anyway it doesn't hurt and makes me look more rufty tufty. I may even have done it on one of my adventures. I really don't know.

Anyway we were all dog tired from

The Secret Adventures of Rolo

the sea air and I slept like a log in my basket. Hope it stays dry for more adventures tomorrow. Wonder how Athelstan and the small folk are coping without me. The people are sleeping on the settees so I'm seizing the moment to blog.

Dog blog #19 According to Rolo

Well this morning I was bundled into the car — first time in 3 days! Only a short journey though; a bit twisty turny round the bends but at least I am a Jack Russell of robust constitution (except where seawater is concerned).

We didn't go far; only to Salcombe. I spent a few hours on the lead — the grown-ups were smug that the car park machine was out of order and no one was bothering with

The Secret Adventures of Rolo

buying tickets so they parked for free. I sat at the smiley lady's feet overlooking the marina and did my best meerkat impression, but she didn't share any of her Salcombe crab sandwich with me (she kept going on about how it was the best she'd ever had) — well how would I know? Then they had Salcombe Dairy honeycomb ice cream, the last of the season before the shop shut up as it was the end of half-term holidays.

Still nothing coming my way. All the dogs I met today were kept on leads. We were going to catch the little ferry across to the sandy beach opposite for a run around but a big black cloud appeared so we drove around there instead.

I haven't yet learned that all

clear water isn't necessarily drinkable — so I gulped some more seawater and then to my surprise it suddenly reappeared. We stopped at South Milton Sands and that was fun — some new dogs to chase, the wind under my tail, and kite surfers to watch, wrestling to control their giant wings in the blustery winds.

Back to The Sloop this evening. The smiley lady was banging on about it being the only pub that does fish pie, and although they'd made a big one yesterday, she was feeling pessimistic... supposing a coach party had come in at lunchtime and eaten the lot? Gloom and doom.

But she was in luck. Not many dogs under the tables this evening. A strange little girl crawled up to me on all fours and spoke in a baby voice. I humoured her, but it wasn't that exciting. I didn't even mind when she jabbed her fingers in my mouth. I was very gentle. They promise me long romps tomorrow, weather permitting!

Dog blog #20 According to Rolo

I have really enjoyed my first seaside holiday in South Devon. Talking to the other dogs, it seems that it is a sort of puppy club in the pub — if we all sit quietly and don't bark or fight we will be allowed to partake...in the pub atmosphere if not the food and drink.

I had a few more romps in the sea — started showing off and playing 'dare' with a big Labrador and nearly ended up out of my depth and had to be rescued. Yes, well, how embarrassing...we'll gloss over that one.

We walked across the causeway to Burgh Island, which we rechristened Snooty Island because of the very unfriendly sign on the Pilchard Inn pub, about it being open to residents and locals only, of which we were neither.

Sunday morning was bright and sunny and I got the grown-ups out of bed and we walked through Thurlestone Golf Course and over the cliffs for the last time;lovely autumn colours and crisp sunshine. We then spent 2 and a half hours in the car which seemed an awfully long drive, and went into a lovely dog friendly pub called The Bull at Hinton, unbeknown to me, back in Wiltshire.

As I sat under the table I thought to myself, this is a very long way to come to the pub…are we going all that way back again? But of course not, we were nearly home. There was a smattering of white stuff on the hills; enough to get the floppy haired boy excited when he flew back from the warmer climate where he had spent his half term holiday - surely the promise of winter adventures to come!

So here I am, back home, running over the fields and drinking muddy puddles, though the smiley lady puts me on a lead when we get near the farmer's fields beyond poo alley, as there are lots of young pheasants and grouse all having been reared and released for sport. That doesn't involve me chasing them apparently. The blackbirds chatter as they scatter and the Red Kite hovers overhead. Anyway I'm looking forward to seeing Athelstan and being sent on my next adventure!

Oops, better go; the floppy haired boy nearly caught me using his laptop!

Chapter 14

Understory Adventure – Rolo to the Rescue in the Blitz

Da's country wisdom for November: "A cold November means a warm Christmas." Many trees can now be identified by their outline. If we have had rain, wind and a touch of frost they will have lost all but the last few leaves. Alder and hazel already show catkins.

Moles begin to make fresh runs; the tell-tale mound of a molehill is the finest sifted soil as they burrow deeper underground for warmth. Green shoots of winter wheat may break the surface of the brown field, and hedging and ditching is the seasonal occupation of the farmer. Most mammals have now settled down to take their long winter sleep. Newts, toads and frogs seek their winter retreat in the murky depths of pond and stream. You might surprise a field mouse or squirrel having a secret snack from its larder hoard. If you are really lucky you might witness a murmuration when starlings flock and swoop in huge numbers, all turning mid-air as one; the noise is incredible. Keep your eyes and ears open.

Dog blog #21 According to Rolo

Firework night and there were loud bangs in the night sky echoing over the garden. The smiley lady and the boy with floppy hair looked out of the window, oohing and ah-ing over the bright bursts of colour. They kept me indoors and drew the curtains, turning the telly up as they thought I would be scared. I wasn't scared; I was ANGRY! I don't like loud noises on MY patch.

212

A brief conversation with Athelstan went something like this:

"As you are a rescued pup, it is fitting that you become a rescuer. You showed your mettle helping the cat in the Fire; now there is more serious work to be done."

Emerging from the tunnel and waving off the tiny lamp bearers, I nearly bolted back down the hole after them. There were lots of loud bangs and fireworks lighting up the sky. Only they weren't fireworks – not the brightly coloured ones the floppy haired boy lights to celebrate Guy Fawkes Night at the beginning of November anyway. (I'm not scared of fireworks by the way, just angry about them. How dare people let them off in my garden?)

No – these were seriously loud bangs and I WAS scared. Suddenly the noise stopped and I could smell smoke. I ran about yapping as I don't like fire. There were sirens going off and that nearly sent me crazy – I don't even like it when the floppy haired

The Secret Adventures of Rolo

boy leaves the fridge open and it beeps. Then a man in a white tin helmet that said ARP on it caught me by the collar and said,

"Are you a rescue dog? Come quickly. We need you over here."

I could see there was a commotion. Something terrible had happened. I followed where he pointed. We found ourselves standing next to the remains of a building which had just become a mass of rubble. There was dust everywhere and I could hear faint cries coming from the pile of bricks. It was very faint and I doubted the humans could hear the distress sound.

A woman in a raincoat and headscarf was sobbing frantically as she tried to explain to anyone who would listen that her son was trapped somewhere underneath that lot. A fire bomb from a German plane had brought the whole lot down. Without hesitation, I scampered over the damaged bricks and disappeared from view down a hole opened up by the explosion. I followed not only the sound but also the scent. 'This could be my floppy haired boy trapped under here,' I thought, and that thought drove me on with no care for my own personal safety. Wheezing slightly I gritted my teeth, and scrabbling with my front paws like a creature possessed, I pressed on. This was a tough job. The sound of sobbing was getting louder. I'd found the lad, but he was trapped. There were all kinds of bricks and rubble on top of him.

The boy was frightened, although I did not think too badly hurt, just stuck. I snuggled into him and licked his face and he responded by blinking and moving his arms a bit. This encouraged me. I struggled back

215

out the way I had come. This is difficult for a terrier, because rather than turn round, we tend to shuffle backwards and put our forelegs outwards to assist with movement; although in reality this makes us wider and therefore means retreating from a hole the way we came in is much more difficult. Nothing we can do about it...it's the way we Jack Russells are made.

There was no room to turn round in this bomb devastation. I started barking to show the rescuers where the boy was located and backed out white flag tail first, sneezing into the daylight of the rubble strewn street. The head-scarved woman fell into a faint and was attended to by kindly tea-bearing neighbours, and the ARP warden bent down and patted me and then immediately got to work with a shovel and a team of volunteers to try to gently dig the boy out of the rubble to safety without causing him anymore harm.

I heard that his name was Nick. His mother had recovered from her faint and, restored by the tea, she engulfed him as he was carried to the surface on a makeshift stretcher with luckily only minor injuries. I slipped away from the scene when I heard Nick ask his mum if they could keep me.

She pointed out that they didn't have a home anymore and burst into tears again. Anyway, I belonged to another floppy haired boy, but they couldn't know that of course. Roaming around the bombed out streets I met a few other rescue dogs, tirelessly assisting ARP wardens in their continual search for trapped bomb victims.

All kinds of dogs were helping out: Alsatians, terriers, collies, wire haired fox terriers; any dog that could follow a scent would be invaluable seeking out life where human rescuers could not, and many wartime household pets were also rescued by these loyal canines. By the time I found my way back to the time tunnel I could barely see because I had tears in my eyes. Most unusual for me. It must be the smoke and dust. Harrumph.

"Are you alright Paddy Paws?" asked Yulia with concern in her voice. I assured her I was and followed her in a sombre mood through the time tunnel. I went home slightly less full of my own self-importance and a lot quieter than usual. A humbling lesson had been learned.

Athelstan gave me the full facts of the Blitz the next time we met. He told me that the people of London had suffered terrible bombing night after night from 7th September 1940 until May 1941, as the German Luftwaffe tried to literally blast the city into submission with their relentless air raids. It became part of everyday life to sleep in either a specially constructed Andersen Shelter, or more latterly, by crowding onto the platforms of the London Underground system.

The night time raids were the worst. The whole capital became sleep-deprived, but Londoners are a stoic breed; they did not give in to despair. Even King George VI and Queen Elizabeth refused to leave London not wanting to desert their loyal subjects nor show signs of cowardice. Eventually Hitler found another target, Russia, and the bombing of London and other cities ceased. 1.4 million people had been made homeless across Britain, but it would be another four years before the war ended.

I slept for a few hours and then we had our usual walk and then the lady put on the television (most unusual for her to do that in the morning) and she sat teary eyed watching the Remembrance Day service from Whitehall. If only she knew what I'd been up to the previous night – or was it more than 60 years ago? I wonder what became of the bombed out boy and his mother.

Dog blog #22 According to Rolo

The floppy haired boy has gone upstairs leaving his laptop in the lounge so here I am...

Just been out for a lovely walk

along the beech hedge which borders the whole length of the field we know as Poo Alley. We were both surprised to hear shots and immediately I thought I was back in the Second World War.

Realising it was the 21st century, however, we were both even more surprised when two young female deer shot out from the hedge and raced the whole length of the field, no doubt startled by the gun fire. The lady put me back on the lead. I wanted to chase after the deer because they looked to be having so much fun bounding over the stubble of the summer wheat, but the men were shooting grouse and pheasants and the smiley lady obviously thought it might be a bit dangerous to walk that way this morning.

Little did she know what I'd
been through in my night time
adventures! We altered our route
and walked a different path.
Past the owl tree. No sign of my
messenger friend this morning.
Probably sleeping. Lucky owl.

Da's country wisdom for December: "If sun shines through apple trees upon a Christmas Day, the following autumn they will a load of fruit display"

As the year grows older, the nights grow longer and when the blackbird rises late he chatters like an angry old man. Holly is cheerful with red berries, and mistletoe in apple trees is full of round white berries like snowballs.

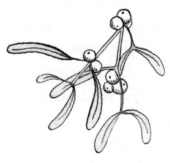

221

Most of the thrush family love berries and a heavy crop predicts a hard winter ahead. Brown owls hoot, foxes bark and deer bray. Night time noises will be muffled if there is snow on the ground.

A jay can be seen, a large fleeting purple coloured shadow. Small birds shelter in the thickets of the hedgerows: chaffinches, greenfinches, sparrows. The solitary robin is still fiercely marking his territory through loud vocals. As the year turns, Nature begins her cycle all over again, year in year out, down the centuries we only have to be still for a moment and look and listen in wonder.

Dog blog #23 According to Rolo

Quick update whilst no-one's looking.

The smiley lady's friend, the jolly lady who loves Jack Russells, is back in town! They had a girly day lunching, chatting and shopping in Devizes and naturally I was dragged along. Lots of interesting walls

The Secret Adventures of Rolo

and posts to sniff, and a market to explore, and all was going well until I got tied to an advertising board on an 'A' frame and left outside a shop for a little while.

I know it's not manly or big but I cried. A lot. And when the lady came out to comfort me whilst the jolly lady was still queuing at the till, I seized my chance, slipped the lead and ran inside the big automatic doors which went swoosh to let me in.

Oooooh, it was exciting! I dodged around the hardware store and everyone was smiling and laughing and the normally smiley lady was running round like a headless chicken waving the lead and trying to catch me, in this 'no dogs allowed' shop. The shop workers were lovely and friendly and eventually I ran up to the lady's jolly friend and thought I was so clever to find her in the chaos. She held me firmly by the collar. I was once again attached to my lead. Shops are such fun! Then we went to The Bear Hotel for lunch and I was allowed in the Market Bar. Whilst my smiley lady and the Jolly lady chatted and chatted and chatted over an early Christmas dinner, I was ignored.

I sat quietly under the table and met a poodle in a coat, and then a smaller Jack Russell. I made polite conversation and was admired greatly. Because I was such a good boy, the jolly lady slipped a bit of turkey under the table. Mmmmmm, I'm looking forward to Christmas!

The boy with floppy hair has taught me a dance called Gangnam Style...or should that be Rolo style? I think he wants to go on Britain's Got Talent with me. Dancing Dog with Teenager? Who would ever think of such a thing?

A lovely forest-smelling fresh tree has suddenly appeared in the lounge. Everyone keeps telling me it's not a wee-ing post...as if I would, in my own home! I'm far better mannered than that! It has pretty lights on it and a scary fairy on the top. Every time someone leans round the tree to turn the lights on or off, or to draw the curtains, hundreds of little green needles fall onto the carpet.

The smiley lady seems to be

hoovering more than usual and she
laughs when I retrieve fallen tree
decorations and come out covered in
little spikes.

Dog blog #24 According to Rolo

Hello everyone, Rolo here. Sorry
I've been a bit too preoccupied
to blog lately. The boy with
floppy hair's big brother came to
stay again carrying a mysterious
cardboard box. I thought it was an
early Xmas present for me, but it
got whisked upstairs and the stair
gate firmly closed.

I spent a few days listening from
behind the gate at the top of the
stairs and swear I can detect
some sort of life behind the door
which is always shut. Then some
of the lady's other friends came

to stay which meant they needed
that bedroom and there was a
huge operation to put me out in
the garden whilst the box was
transported to the conservatory.
The floppy haired boy built some
kind of playground with pallets and
I still couldn't quite work out
what was going on.

Then the secret guest broke for
freedom and made it over the
playground wall, still in the
conservatory but with its nose
pressed up against the glass
staring into the lounge. I found
myself face to face with the
MYSTERIOUS RABBIT!!

All my Christmases have surely come
at once!!!!! But they won't let me
out there to play with it, so I sit
behind the curtains with my head

The Secret Adventures of Rolo

on one side, blowing at the patio door as if I can magically will the rabbit this side of the glass.

Today all the guests left, leaving just me and the floppy haired boy, the smiley lady and the rabbit, which is now back upstairs once more contained behind the door of the spare room they now call The Rabbit Room. I took up my position at the top of the stairs, restrained only by the 'stare' gate (as it has now been rechristened).

The floppy haired boy had a brainwave to move the gate down stairs so now I can only sit on the bottom step very quietly and wonder what kind of party the three of them are having up there without me. Let the Jack Russell see the rabbit I say!

The Secret Adventures of Rolo

N.B. I overheard the smiley lady say to the floppy haired boy, "If that rabbit is still alive by New Year it will be a miracle." Why is that? Is there something wrong with it I wonder? Does it have health issues? Can I be of some assistance?

Right, they're playing a board game…time to do some more blogging…

The day after Christmas and I find myself bundled into my travelling box and we set off by car for Farringdon in Oxfordshire. It's a beautifully sunny but cold day. We parked at a farm. What a sight greeted my eyes! It is a Boxing Day Hunt!

There were a lot of people on horseback, some wearing red coats.

A huge crowd turned out to watch
and there were notices saying
'Please keep your pet dogs away
from the hounds'. The hounds were
big creatures; roaming freely
in the throng and boy did they
look hungry. Several sniffed me
suspiciously. I sensed that these
were working dogs. The Master of
the Hunt made an announcement on
the tanoy system,

"We are hunting legally today
following a previously-laid scented

trail. No foxes will be caught."
I didn't know what that meant but
I heard the smiley lady explain to
the floppy haired boy that a trail
could be laid using aniseed or
meat or animal urine soaked into
branches dragged over a pre-planned
course.

Followers of the hunt and the
hounds would follow the scent. The
argument against this from hunt
aficionados was that it set a time
restriction and a planned route on
the hunt, without the spontaneity
of chasing a live animal such as a
fox.

I was kept very firmly on my lead
and told off for pulling. I whined
quite a lot in frustration as I
really wanted to join in the fun. A
hunting horn sounded and the field

went quiet; the horses were being reined in and stomped impatiently. Suddenly, the riders tore off across the field in the same direction and jumped a fence several at a time, clearing a ditch in the corner of the field. Nobody fell off.

The hounds were called to order and I really wanted to join them! I had heard that every pack of hounds has a Jack Russell to keep them in order. I can be bossy; I want to be that dog! Another thing that confused me was the term for the outfit worn by huntsmen and women. The scarlet jackets were referred to as 'hunting pink' and no one could explain why.

It certainly was a breath-taking sight even to this little dog, and steeped in tradition dating back

to the Fifteenth Century. Hunt
followers had found a way around
the Fox Hunting ban of 2004 and
could still get together for a Meet
without incurring the wrath of hunt
saboteurs. They disagreed with it
on the grounds of cruelty to the
fox, whilst supporters consider
the fox to be vermin and saw it as
their duty to control them. All
this I learned from Athelstan who
as you know by now is very wise.

Da's country wisdom for January:
This is the month of doorways and
beginnings. Country folk say that the worst
of winter is yet to come but, despite this,
the gorse on the moors lights a few golden

lamps to welcome in the New Year.
In churchyards, ancient yew, planted to
provide the parish with wood to make bows
or to repel cattle with its poisonous berry,
will blossom and yellow jasmine flowers can
be seen brightening cottage porches and
hazel catkins tremble in the wind. Signs of
new life abound, especially if there has not
yet been a harsh frost.

The robin is a good barometer; if a storm
is coming he will sing from the shelter of
a hedge or bush but if the weather is fair
he will sing out in the open. Skylarks can
be heard singing over fields and the green
woodpecker is laughing his distinctive
'yaffle'.

Pigeons coo and a kestrel hovers overhead.
Small birds vanish for shelter in the maze
of twigs tangled in the hedges. Starlings
swoop over distant fields. Listen out for
the choral skills of the thrushes, blackbird,
wren, robin, hedge sparrow, woodlark,
chaffinch and nuthatch.

Most mammals are still sleeping but rabbits
can be seen, and the occasional hare
although they tend to cling to the safety
of the hedgerow. On the downs, early baby
lambs bleat and are answered by their

deeper voiced mother ewes. The shepherd watches the colour of the sky for a clue as to the weather on the morrow.

Dog Blog #25 According to Rolo

They're both busy having a 'grand tidy up' whatever that means. Sweet wrappers from down the back of the settees I suspect.

Early in January, the rabbit disappeared (alive, I hasten to add.) The tree in the lounge also mysteriously went (not so alive) and the smiley lady rearranged the furniture to cover up the needles still stubbornly clinging to the wool carpet despite her best efforts at vacuuming. I always fight with the vacuum cleaner and usually get put out in the garden when she wields it around the house.

It's a big and noisy grey and orange monster and I try to sneak up on it by running at the long pipe with the brush on the end and biting it. I don't know why this stops the lady smiling or why she puts me outside. It's just a game we play, the monster and I.

The floppy haired boy seemed surprised to be back at school already as he had not completed the homework set over the holiday period. I must tell you something really funny while I remember.

The floppy haired boy likes to take my collar off when I'm around the house. He thinks I should be allowed to just be a dog without something hanging round my neck. Mind you, I find it quite useful to be wearing it when they forget

The Secret Adventures of Rolo

to refill my water bowl in the kitchen, because I clank my metal tag against the dish and that's how they know I'm thirsty.

Anyway, this particular morning the smiley lady was running late and was rushing around everywhere looking for my collar, because when the floppy haired boy takes it off, he leaves it wherever he happens to be. It wasn't in any of the usual places, neither in the hallway nor on the arm of the settee, and the smiley lady was getting pretty cross because she was in a big hurry to walk me and then go out to a meeting.

The floppy haired boy had already gone to school so she couldn't ask him where he'd put it. So the not-so-smiley lady made a game of

The Secret Adventures of Rolo

it...'Come on Rolo, lets find your
collar' and led the way all over
the house and I helped her in her
search. I thought it was a great
game. After about 20 minutes she
gave up, and retrieved my old
collar from a nail in the garage
and bent down to fasten it around
my neck, and then she collapsed
in a heap on the floor, rocking
from side to side and laughing her
head off. I was already wearing my
collar!

Now she thinks I'm incredibly
intelligent, that I found my collar
where the floppy haired boy had left
it and put it on myself ready for
my walk. She laughed so much she
was crying...although she did make
some remark about my Christmas
chins hiding the collar...cheeky
lady...look in the mirror! You and

the floppy haired boy both...

I found myself travelling in the car with the smiley lady on an adventure to a little place called Haxey, where you may recall I fetched a lady's bonnet, back in the 13th century.

More about this later as I don't want to be caught blogging!

Right, back again...

A bit of background information for you; the village of Haxey stands on the edge of North Lincolnshire where it borders South Yorkshire. Before this fenland area was drained in the 17th century, the area was known as the Isle of Axholme, full of dykes, ditches and marshes, a very boggy place indeed. We were visiting the smiley lady's lively librarian friend who is Haxey born and bred. As they sat chatting waiting for more revellers to arrive, I set about investigating my new surroundings with some polite sniffing. I overheard the lively librarian explaining the story of The Haxey Hood to the smiley lady, and it went something like this:

In early January during the 13th century, the local landowner's wife, Lady de Mowbray, was out riding on a blustery day and her silk bonnet blew off and was carried by the gusting wind, travelling over several ditches and fields to the amusement and concern of the 13 workers who were tending the land. The men immediately gave chase and frolicked after the rogue hood

240

which seemed to have a life of its own as it soared over hedges and led them laughing through muddy ditches. Lady de Mowbray thought this was all great sport and she was delighted when her hood was finally captured by the biggest but shyest of the men, who asked someone else to approach her with the retrieved sodden hood.

She promised each of the 13 workers a portion of land if they could devise a game which would re-enact the antics of the chasing of the hood. She called the men 'Plough Boggins' and they would play an important role as marshals in the first Haxey Hood, and when the game was discussed, the catcher was named The Fool and he would henceforth wear harlequin, and The Lord was the man who handed the bonnet to the lady.

The smiley lady learned from her friend that this was probably the oldest and longest running traditional revelry in England. She was fascinated.

To this very day, the folks of Haxey assemble from noon on the Church green on 6th January every year (unless that is a Sunday in which case held on the Saturday) to partake in, or witness the mass chase of a replica hood.

And that is why we were here on this particular January afternoon. The lively librarian went on to further explain that what actually happened at the modern day 'Hood' was that the bells would peal at 2pm and the 'Lord' (a notable local) and his elected 'Boggins' all dressed in brightly coloured clothes, would process down the street and the Fool would make a speech to welcome the revellers (many now travel from far and wide) and set the challenge. The Lord would then lead everyone to the highest point of the surrounding area and the Boggins would make a circle.

The Lord would throw a replica of the hood into the air and it is up to any youngster to try to catch it and run away with it but if he is tackled he must throw it up in the air again. If a Boggin catches it, it is 'boggined' (a local word meaning returned to the Lord). Anyone who manages to capture and keep the hood could then turn it in for a reward at the end of a session of play. Then the serious game would begin among the adults, and this was more of a rugby scrum between sometimes as many as several hundred people, fighting over the hood. The idea was for one of the competing teams to capture the hood and carry it over the threshold of their local pub where it would be displayed with pride for the next twelve months. It was a hard fought competition with no holds barred.

Players enjoyed the rule of 'No Law' which meant there was no such thing as trespass and they could go anywhere whilst playing the game.

The Boggins played the role of referees and also encouraged onlookers to join in. The smiley lady was keen to have a go although the lively librarian advised her against it. Anyway, when other friends arrived with a very well behaved black Labrador, we set out to witness this historic event first hand. I really wanted to tell them that I'd actually been the one to retrieve the original bonnet, but of course I couldn't tell them anything, so instead I played politely with the Labrador and was kept on a short lead because of the lively but good natured crowd.

I was alarmed when the smiley lady handed the lead over to the lively librarian and dived headlong into the approaching melee. She was soon on the ground and strong arms hauled her back to her feet and out of the scrum. Needless to say she retreated rather sheepishly and said she'd had a go and that was enough!

Well, silly people. If only they knew the truth about the origins of the game!

A few weeks later, the smiley lady went wassailing with the Community Choir (aha! Now I know what Athelstan's very first greeting to me meant!). Surprisingly she took me along because she decided I'm as much a part of the community as she is. This was quite exciting as we started off in the Priory Gardens where I am not usually allowed to go. Basically we were singing to the apple trees at various points around the town and encouraging them to give good fruit by pouring cider on their roots. The bishop was in attendance and the choir sang a wassailing song at every stop.

This was the revival of an old tradition. The inhabitants of Marlborough would then bang pots and pans to drive away the bad spirits as well as scatter crumbs for the birds who were the keepers of the apple trees. Now that bit I could relate to, knowing Athelstan. Don't think he'd be too impressed with stale bread though! Anyway, I didn't like it when they banged saucepans with wooden spoons and every time the din started up I jumped into the smiley lady's arms, much to the amusement of her fellow singers and assembled crowd.

When it was all over, we processed to St Mary's Church for some mulled cider. I was allowed inside the church with it being a special occasion and was even blessed by the Bishop of Ramsbury, who also gave me a biscuit when no one was looking! Now I am a holy dog.

Whilst the smiley lady was chatting with the assembled townsfolk and choir people outside the porch, I had the opportunity of viewing the fire-scorched stonework and the rather weathered carving of the cat that had allegedly saved her kittens during the Great Fire in 1653. The stone carving is rather high up on the parapet next to the tower and it takes a lot of imagination to work out what it's supposed to be!

Hang on a minute! Where's my likeness? Not even a mention of the brave Jack Russell who fearlessly dove into the flames time and time again to save those pesky kittens! The smiley lady literally had to

The Secret Adventures of Rolo

drag me away from the church. I was that cross! On the way home we passed number 105 The High Street and there I spied a wooden carving on a decorative door of the same cat rescuing her kittens, with the date of the fire — again no reference to me!

I am an unremarkable hero — sigh. The smiley lady wondered what was wrong with me as she had to drag me along the High Street and all the

The Secret Adventures of Rolo

way home. Unfortunately I couldn't tell her why I was sulking.

That evening I did 'clown eyes' at the floppy haired boy, much to his delight. I was dreaming of castles.

Da's country wisdom for February: "If Candlemas Day (2nd February) be fair and bright, winter will have another flight; if Candlemas Day be cloud and rain, then winter will not come again."

February is sometimes called the gateway of the year and the snowdrop lights the path with tiny white lamps. Male blackbirds with sleek glossy plumage fight over their chosen mate. Coltsfoot yellow flowers appear along the bank even before their leaves. Young nettles push their way through even the hardest of earth. Early celandines peep through and the pink tips of the daisy flower are a welcome sight. Willow trees unfold their silver catkins and lapwings are pairing with incredible aerobatic displays; their distinctive cry of 'pee wit' ringing out. The song thrush becomes more melodic as the days lengthen. Listen out for a yellow hammer crying out for 'a little bit o' bread and no che-e-se'.

Moles are active; you will see the fresh
molehills breaking out of even the best
manicured lawn. Moles apparently work for
three hours and then rest for three hours,
not distinguishing between day and night time.
Blackbirds, house sparrows, herons, rooks,
magpies, ravens, starlings and tawny owls
will all begin nesting this month – Valentine's
Day being the traditional time to choose a
mate in the bird world.

The Secret Adventures of Rolo

Chapter 15

Understory Adventure – Rolo Investigates Marlborough Castle

During our next night time meeting, Athelstan told me what he knows of the big hill known locally as Marlborough Mound. The wise keeper of the forest says that there has been some sort of castle on the top of the Mound since the time of William the Conqueror (which my historical knowledge tells me is 1066). Athelstan said that the castle grew up initially not as a serious means of defence, but more a Royal hunting lodge close to deer-rich Savernake Forest.

What puzzled me was how it went from being possibly the fourth most important castle in England, visited and lived in by Henry l, Henry ll and Henry lll, and given as a wedding gift by King Richard l to his brother John (he of Magna Carta fame) along with neighbouring and now ruined Ludgershall Castle, to having completely disappeared? Prince John was even married in the chapel of Marlborough Castle dedicated to St Nicholas. He later became King John. All of this information I eagerly absorbed.

The smiley lady would be impressed as she loves history, but of course I can't share any of this with her. Anyway, I was keen to visit the once prestigious castle. This wouldn't really need the use of the secret tunnel being located so close to where I live, but of course I would be travelling to a different era… and wait, it's not just a tree-topped mound in the grounds of Marlborough College as visible from the A4 in the 21st Century! Athelstan's wise words are still echoing in my head as I scamper out from the time tunnel:

"This Mound has the same air of mystery about its origins as nearby Silbury Hill; both are similar in appearance and were constructed around 2400BC and possibly have something to do with the worship of water goddesses due to both mounds' proximity to underground springs. Glad to see you take such an interest in local history little pup." I can see the walls of a castle and I bound up the hill to investigate.

The year was 1204 and medieval castle life was in full swing. There were a lot of people within the castle walls; some were shepherding animals, some were repairing walls; there were travelling entertainers, cooks, soldiers and servants. There was a flurry of activity and an air of importance as King John was within and dictating a royal charter to a weary clerk.

A charter was a legal document confirming the rights of the townsfolk to be guaranteed by the monarch. The reason for this decree was to increase the King's popularity in the towns which had proved loyal to him. Marlborough remains very proud of its charter which still stands today (Athelstan told me so).

But back to 1204…the castle is not the original motte-and-bailey Norman build of old; it has been reinforced with stone and King John has overseen the building of a retaining wall around the mound and a barbican tower overlooking the drawbridge. This was now more of a defensive castle complete with moat and artillery store. King John's hold over the country was rather tenuous and it seemed sensible for him to fortify his castles in case he needed to defend his right to be king. Roofs were repaired and windows installed and houses restored which meant in turn the town itself prospered and grew in the shadow of the castle. By all accounts King John was a good, if often absent landlord.

There was a roaring fire burning in the huge stone fire place, and wool tapestries depicting mythological scenes were hanging over the windows to keep out the draughts.

Castles were cold and rather dark places and I managed to sneak in front of the big open fire to warm myself, laying down flat on the sweet smelling rushes and trying very hard not to be noticed. King John was striding about, waving his arms and trying to come up with some kind of promises to reward the townspeople, and every word he spoke was being carefully written down by his clerk, a young lad whom I thought resembled the floppy haired boy.

Suddenly King John stopped pacing around the room, turned on his heel abruptly with his cloak billowing out behind him and excused himself for a moment, banging the door on his way out waking up the sleepy sentries who were supposed to be standing guard to the royal personage.

The weary clerk laid down his quill and stood up to stretch his limbs and rub his hands in front of the fire. That's when he noticed me. He bent down to tickle my ears and I rolled over to give him access to my tummy.

"Where did you spring from young hound?" I knew he was the floppy haired boy! He started speaking and I took the chance of answering him, not sure if he would be able to hear me or not. These people all seem to talk to themselves! He was wondering what the people of Marlborough would really want granted in their town charter. The towns of

The Secret Adventures of Rolo

Oxford and Hoyland had been easy to sort out. Now this clerk would accompany the King and his retinue, around the countryside thinking up ways of placating the townsfolk of other places to keep them loyal to the crown.

"A regular market," I said out loud.

"What did you say little hound?" he bent down and ruffled my ears a bit more, not quite believing what he thought he had heard. Now I don't know how some folks can hear me speak and others can't, but then I don't really understand how I can time travel either. I don't worry about the logistics of this kind of thing. Just enjoy the adventure.

"A regular market…and a fair," I added, "and the right of way through the town." I was in my element now, and the clerk was scratching his head incredulously.

"Oh, and a plaque to honour a very important dog placed above a permanent doggy water bowl in the

The Secret Adventures of Rolo

High Street." I thought perhaps I'd gone too far but nothing ventured, nothing gained as they say. I had nothing to lose and was enjoying the experience.

At that moment, King John strode back into the room calling for a cup of mead and the door banged shut behind him with a resounding thud.

"Now where was I?" he bellowed. The bemused clerk took up his quill and, bowing before he spoke, timidly suggested a twice weekly market and an annual fair for the townsfolk of Marlborough, something that had not been offered to the previous towns visited.

"Splendid idea. I must have been thinking out loud!" said the King. "Write it down; we'll formalise the

The Secret Adventures of Rolo

charter when we get to Winchester."

The clerk gave a weary little sigh. He never received any credit for his ideas. Wait a minute – they were MY ideas! The rest of my suggestions went unsaid and were therefore not included in the charter of 1204.

When I returned through the time tunnel, I asked Athelstan what had happened to the magnificent castle, as there is nothing of it visible today.

The gatekeeper replied: "After King John, Henry lll spent a lot of time in the castle and much building work was done. The town itself grew in importance and stature along with the fine royal castle which by now had its own mint. Remember that coin you brought me from Peter Long? That was a 'Maerleber' minted here in the castle's heyday.

In 1267 the castle witnessed an historic event of some importance when the King faced the barons in a row over the Statute of Marlborough and the reigning monarch was once more forced to address his subjects' grievances.

Certainly by the end of the next century the old castle had fallen out of royal favour and into ruin. By the 19th century no trace of the castle or its fine stonework remained. The Belgian black marble font now found in St George's Church, Preshute (thought to be the oldest church in Marlborough) came from the castle chapel of St Nicholas."

Thinking about it, the fine font is way too grand to have been commissioned for an ordinary parish church. I have been inside St George's when the smiley lady went practising with the choir. Athelstan went on to say that if you climb the tower of St Peter's Church, you can look down on the town of Marlborough and see many stones that were pinched from the castle having been absorbed into the townsfolk's boundary walls and buildings.

The castle has simply disappeared over time and its fabric has filtered into the town's buildings.

"The Seymour family in Tudor times inherited the ruin and the land it stood on, and built a fine house which became the nucleus of Marlborough College, but you will discover that on another adventure," he finished.

At this point it is worth noting to my readers that there is still no permanent dog bowl with commemorative plaque in the High Street. 'Harrumph' as Da would say.

Dog blog #26 According to Rolo

Both people are busy and the laptop is left unattended. A quick catch up...

Something most peculiar happened this morning: it's weird when something you witnessed 500 years ago catches up with you, but I suppose that's one of the hazards of time travelling.
The smiley lady took me down to the High Street to buy a newspaper. I

261

like this kind of outing, because, despite being kept on the lead, a lot of people stop her in the street to remark on what a handsome dog I am. As you know by now, I love the attention.

This particular morning, the smiley lady bumped into one of her singing friends, a lovely kind lady who immediately invited us in for coffee. She had recently moved into a townhouse in the shadow of St Peter's church and was having a conservatory built outside to give her extra living space. She was explaining the plans to the smiley lady and I was offered a biscuit. This pleased me greatly; these were fancy sweet biscuits. I accepted politely. Anyway, as the ladies chatted I went off to explore.

"Just off for a bite of lunch Mrs; back at two o'clock," shouted the cheery builders as they traipsed through the house in their big dirty boots luckily keeping to the confines of the carefully laid plastic sheeting. I thought I'd nip out the back and inspect their work, fancying myself as a bit of a foreman.

They had dug the foundations, and far from being all chalk, as you might have expected, I was surprised to find layers of mud. It looked easy to dig and I thought I'd help them a bit. I went to work digging frantically with my front paws, using all my concentration.

"What is it Rolo? What have you found?" called the smiley lady from the window. She was saying to the kind lady that she would love to have a metal detector so she could go excavating for Roman coins and other buried treasure, and how fascinating if historical objects could tell a story. Hahaha, I laughed to myself! Little did she know that she doesn't really need a metal detecting device to dig up history with me around! Anyway, I kept on digging away, and both ladies came out into the garden to see what I was up to.

I finally managed to tease it out — it was a ring with a big ruby coloured stone set in it. And what's more I knew exactly where it had come from and how it got there. A bit more frantic scrabbling on my part revealed a few more items of jewellery, too, and a couple of coins and a silver goblet. Both ladies were very excited and soon took over the excavation. Then the kind lady went indoors to phone the local newspaper. The smiley lady thought they were possibly Tudor artefacts. 'Spot on, smiley lady,' I thought, but of course I couldn't tell her. I did get my photograph in the newspaper though — at least the kind lady in the High Street credited me with the find! And now the smiley lady keeps making jokes about not needing a metal detector with me around. The funny thing is the guards obviously never did come back to dig up their buried treasure. I wonder whatever happened to Reynold and Percy. I don't suppose I'll ever find out.

Da's country wisdom for March: "A wet March means a sad harvest."

The Secret Adventures of Rolo

Clocks spring forward; this is the lengthening month bringing longer daylight hours and the promise of better weather to come.

Wild daffodils bob their pretty heads and curtsey in the spring wind.

Daisies and dandelions add colour to the grass. On the floor of the forest, wood anemones bow their white heads. The flower doesn't open fully until the wind blows strong and this heralds the arrival of the swallow.

It is said that wood anemones curl their petals at sundown to keep their fairy inhabitants safe and snug. The sycamore and horse chestnut unfurl their new growth and sticky buds will break out, and hedgerows will be studded with little points of green shoots. All birds nest this month. Hares are visible as they go a little mad with love and can often be seen chasing one other. The male jacks fight almost to the death over the love of a doe.

Wild rabbits are busy with their young and seek the sanctuary of ploughed fields. Bat, dormouse and hedgehog awaken from their winter rest and even the earthworm is active. (Did you know that earthworms eat their body weight in food every day?) Toads and frogs spawn. Spiders reappear and early butterflies may emerge on sunny days. The warmth of the sunshine draws them out.

Nature spotters see what you can spy in spring.

Chapter 16

Understory Adventure; Rolo and the Hot Air Balloon

"Another BIG adventure!" said Yulia by way of greeting and off we went down the time tunnel, hard to find as the base of the tree was covered with Spring's new growth. 'I hope it's not another one like Pompeii,' I thought to myself. Little did I know this was going to be even more of an adventure!

I couldn't wait to exit the time tunnel and hardly took any notice of where the entrance was. I certainly had a spring in my step. Where on earth was I this time?

It is September 1783 and I am in the grounds of the Royal Palace at Versailles, on the outskirts of Paris. A large crowd has assembled but they are not looking at me. There is what looks like a large laundry basket standing in the middle of the courtyard and this is the focus of their attention.

Being a very curious Jack Russell I can't help but peer in. Bizarrely there is a duck, a sheep and a rooster huddled in the corner of the wicker basket and all are clearly terrified. I can smell their fear. The murmur from the crowd rises in pitch to an audible buzz of anticipation.

"What on earth are you all doing?" I asked the Rooster, who seemed to be quaking marginally less than his strange companions.

"I believe we are about to allez oop in the air pour le Roi et la Reine," spluttered the Rooster, not at all surprised that I could communicate with him. I didn't really know what he meant, but felt it was impolite to say so. He spoke with a French accent similar to that of De Grys the greyhound from my first adventure.

"Don't zay know Roosters can't fly?" he went on. "I'm here entirely for zat reason…zay want to see what will happen to me at altitude. Apparently zee King wanted to use human prisoners for zees

experiment but zee inventors overruled zee king.
Can you imagine?"

The duck piped up in a high pitched voice probably
due to nerves, "I can fly, of course, but using my
wings, not in this unnatural contraption."

The sheep just bleated, rolling its eyes and looked
rather sick.

"Don't mind her," said the rooster. "She's here
because she's called Montauciel, which you Engleesh
would translate as 'climb to the sky' – that's a laugh;
just look at her!" I thought he was being rather
unkind and tactfully changed the subject. The poor
sheep was obviously cacking itself.

"What exactly are you standing in?" I asked, my
nosiness finally getting the better of me I peered into
the large oblong basket.

"Why don't you hop in and regardez for yourself?
There's space for another passenger if we all squash
up a bit," the rooster invited, "the more the merrier".

Without further ado I jumped in the basket, causing the duck to flap its wings and the sheep to bleat even more pathetically.

"Clear the decks!" said the Rooster importantly, stamping around and making room.

The roar of the crowd reached a crescendo and all gave a collective sigh and broke into applause. Suddenly the ground seemed to give way beneath us. The floor didn't seem too steady at all. There was an almighty whooshing sensation and a lot of swaying from side to side. The occupants of the basket bumped into each other as we tried to steady ourselves.

"Zut alors!" shrieked the Rooster. The duck quacked and the sheep just went on bleating. We seemed to be gaining height and I was feeling very wobbly on my little legs. Finally my legs stopped shaking, and I put my front paws on the side of the basket and peered over the rim. I wanted to see what was going on below. Oops I shouldn't have done that!

We lurched a little to the left with the shift of weight.
Quickly jumping back down on the floor of the
basket I reported my sightings to the others.
"Well we seem to be airborne!" I exclaimed and all
four of us looked up to the heavens.

Above us was a rather large and colourful inflated
bag. There was a roar of flames which seemed to
encourage the bag to rise even higher dragging the
basket with it, and we hung for a while precariously

The Secret Adventures of Rolo

hovering over the assembled French court. I peered over the rim again and spied two very important personages wearing tall and elaborate wigs and very fine clothes, seated on thrones on a raised platform. These were presumably the French royalty, Louis XVl and his Queen Marie Antoinette, in the days before they became unpopular with the masses who wanted their heads.

I felt the urge to wave but instead made an important observation, pointing out to my terrified companions that the basket was actually tethered to the ground by a rope and that as we had taken up all the slack we wouldn't be able to rise any higher. "Unless of course the rope breaks," I added mischievously.

At this point the duck looked a little green and the sheep was sick. The rooster pretended it was just a daily event to be taken in his stride. After less than nine minutes of floating to a height of around 1,500 feet, we were gently pulled down to the ground by people manning the rope and the crowd cheered.

273

The fire under the balloon canopy was extinguished. The basket tipped over as we touched down and we all tumbled out, in a heap of tangled wings and legs, as it happened, none the worse for our airborne adventure. Someone asked who 'le chien' was. I presumed that was me and wanted to give my name. Surely we had taken part in an historic event; the very first manned (or should that be 'animaled'?) balloon flight. I pointed this out to the others but they didn't seem very impressed.

As it was only the 18th century, no one took our photos nor interviewed us for a live television news broadcast. Ah well, time to find the tunnel again. Amazing that I could not only travel back in time but to other countries as well! What adventures I could have!

But wait! Where was the tunnel entrance? I couldn't remember where it was. I didn't have a clue how to locate it, didn't recognise anything in the palace grounds and the crowd were milling about flocking towards the exits now the spectacle was over. I got caught up in the thick of it and carried along without any idea if I was heading in the right direction. I started to worry about the time. If I couldn't get back through the time tunnel I wouldn't be back in my basket in the kitchen when the smiley lady came to let me out for my early morning constitutional! No time to panic. Think clearly Rolo.

I decided to hide underneath the stage where the royalty had sat and wait for the crowd to disperse. That seemed the best course of action. I hadn't taken much notice of my surroundings when I popped out in France and really could not remember where the tunnel entrance was.

Darkness descended and a breeze caught a strange shape which started billowing on the ground in front of me. Of course! The discarded balloon! It was lying there still tethered and quite forgotten once the excitement was over. Presumably the Montgolfier brothers would be back in the morning to retrieve it and analyse the success of their flight. If only I could fly the thing I would try to find my way across

the Channel and back home to Wiltshire before
I was missed by my people who would surely be
distraught if I were to go missing!

I sniffed around the balloon and realised that it
was hopeless… I couldn't light the fire to make the
balloon gain height let alone steer it to England!
I settled down to sleep in the basket, dreaming of
my own basket, and, not being given to despair
easily, I felt sure I would think my way out of this
predicament in the morning.

I didn't have to wait that long. An hour or so later,
I heard voices, human voices, and two pony tailed
men approached bearing flaming torches. They
were inspecting the balloon and talking in excited
whispers. I coughed politely and then jumped out of
the basket at their startled feet.

"Excuse me; are you the owners of this balloon?" I
enquired politely to the men with ponytails.

"Jacques did you hear the petit chien speak or am I

The Secret Adventures of Rolo

imagining things?"

"Non, I believe I heard le petit chien speak…are we both going crazy, Joseph? Is it the excitement of the success of our balloon making us hear things, do you think?"

I pressed on. "Excusez-moi. Sorry to startle you, but my name is Rolo and I am in a bit of a fix. Can you fly this balloon?"

The Montgolfier brothers stood opening and closing their mouths like goldfish.

"Actually I'm in a bit of a rush…Si'l vous plait, allez, vite, merci beaucoup," I threw in the only French words I knew. (My limited vocabulary comes from listening to the floppy haired boy's French home tutor.)

Stunned, the brothers had a quick discussion, and I heard a lot of muttering and saw a lot of hand waving. It seemed they had a bit of a dilemma as the

The Secret Adventures of Rolo

King had confiscated the balloon and they had come back to retrieve their property under the secrecy of darkness. Lucky that they had! I know I'm an intelligent dog, but I don't think I could fly it on my own, let alone navigate the way back to the south west of England!

They turned to me, finally in agreement, and gestured to me to hop into the basket once more. Without wasting any more time, Joseph cut the tethering rope with his pocket knife, jumped in the basket with me, using one of their flaming torches to light the burner. Jacques paid out the shortened rope until we started to drift and then he too jumped in. There was something wrong with the burner, however. Jacques jumped out again and pulled on the rope, resulting in a rather bumpy landing.

The brothers' eyes were as round as saucers and their adrenalin was pumping at the thought of such an illicit adventure, and both feared the King's wrath when he discovered the balloon he was pretending to have invented had disappeared. I could hear their

combined heartbeats thumping so loudly in unison
it might appear that the balloon was to be powered
by a motor!

As the brothers worked on the burner apparatus,
I explained my predicament. I needed to go to
southwest England tout de suite and would be very
much obliged if they could assist me. Much to my
surprise, both Joseph and Jacques spoke excellent
English.

Thankfully still under the cover of darkness, the
brothers worked silently and quickly to reassemble
the balloon and the repaired burner to enable us to
escape. Up in the air again we went and this time the
brothers were satisfied with the action of the burner.
Silently and high over the palace walls we flew, and
stealthily across the roof tops of villages and towns
until finally we were above tree tops and at last over
the sea. Just as well it was still night time as anyone
on the ground looking up might have thought
they were seeing a gigantic scary bubble monster
hovering in the sky above them!

The Montgolfiers smiled and nodded and, to pass the time of flight once we had gained altitude, explained to me that their father owned a paper mill and that they had been messing around trying to float little bags in the air made of paper and fabric by way of scientific experiment. The inquisitive brothers had discovered that when they held a candle near the opening of the bag at the bottom, the bag would fill with hot air and rise upwards. They tried to build a larger version out of silk lined with paper and the demonstration of this had gone very well indeed, with the 'balon' reaching a height of over six thousand feet with no one inside it.

Word of their achievement quickly spread to Paris and they were summoned to the French court. Today was only their second attempt at balloon flight and they had secured a light basket and gathered some animals for the journey. They were delighted with how the demonstration had gone, but both were keen to actually ride in the balloon themselves. They thought that the balloon could be modified to carry a number of passengers over great distances. This idea greatly excited them! The trouble was that the King was so impressed by the balon that he had claimed the invention for himself and the Crown had seized the design and forbade the brothers to take home the original model.

The brothers thought this was very unfair and so had sneaked back to Versailles in the night to retrieve their beloved creation. Now it seemed their only chance to put their invention to the human passenger test was to rescue this crazy little English dog and try to fly across the sea with him! I was delighted to have made such good and useful friends. I had really landed on my paws this time! I looked down over the rim of the basket, listening to the roar of the flame which kept us aloft, and the gentle accents of the brothers who were piloting the craft and I couldn't help wondering how they were going to get back to France having dropped me home, and successfully keep their names on their invention. It all seemed rather unfair to me that the King could take all the glory for himself for an idea

The Secret Adventures of Rolo

that wasn't even his in the first place (but it sounded rather familiar if you remember King John and the charter!)

It was very cold at high altitude but I daren't complain; I was just really grateful to be heading home. Joseph took off his thick jacket as he was working up quite a sweat as he wrestled with controlling the power of the flame, and anticipating my needs he laid it on the floor of the basket. I snuggled into it and at last, lulled by the welcome sound of the sea as we crossed the channel, I slept. When I awoke it was already morning and I stretched, feeling for the confines of the wicker basket, similar to my own.

For a moment I had forgotten where I was, and then realised that I was actually on my feet and standing at the bottom of my garden! How on earth did that happen? I didn't think I'd even told the Montgolfier brothers where I lived! No time to ponder that now; no time to lose…I had to get back through the trapdoor quickly…and I had just snuggled myself into my basket when the smiley lady opened the kitchen door with her usual cheery greeting and tummy rub. What was very unusual however was that the floppy haired boy appeared behind her shoulder; his hair tousled and he was rubbing the sleep from his eyes. The smiley lady greeted him, ruffling his hair and saying,

"Hello love, you're up early this morning. What's the matter with you, can't you sleep?" and he replied,

"Mum! Come quick! There's a hot air balloon hovering right over our garden!"

Da's country wisdom for April: "April wet, good wheat."

Poets love April, from Chaucer to T.S. Elliot; the latter wrote rather strangely 'April is 'the cruellest month' but it is surely the freshest to the eye; the countryside is alive with vibrant green new growth. Alternating sunshine and showers brings rainbows and a profusion of wild flowers.

Wild violets can be seen by only the keen-eyed clinging to the banks and wild primroses are the simplest and most beautiful flower.

In quiet meadows, cowslips hang their yellow heads and some trees are already in flower or blossom. Aspen, poplar, balsam, silver birch will all have catkins and elm, beech, larch, lime, maple, walnut, plane, sycamore and ash will all begin to leaf. Returning birds touch down from sunnier winters.

Many birds are nesting. Yellow banded bumble bees can be seen hanging around the newly flowering white dead nettles. Young moles and shrews are born. Squirrels build their 'dreys' (a shabby heap of sticks in the tallest trees; see if you can find one) and toads lay their necklace of eggs. Frog tadpoles can be seen in ponds. Numerous moths emerge and if you are lucky you might see a hedgehog come out at twilight.

Athelstan gave me a bit of a lecture the next evening, with Yulia and her Da and even the owl listening in.

"Rule number one, little pup: never ever forget where the entrance of the time tunnel is. You were very lucky last night. You could still be stuck in France! Poor Yulia and her Da spent hours waiting to light your return. I hope you have learned your lesson and I need you to promise me that you will be more careful in future. Imagine what your people would have done if they found your basket empty? Imagine if you got stuck in another era? There will be no more adventuring for you for a while. Now go home and be a good boy. Make a fuss of your people."

I suddenly felt very small and foolish and apologised sincerely to the tiny woodland folk. Da harrumphed and Yulia stroked my nose so I knew I was forgiven. They were angry because they had been concerned for my safety. That's nice. We rescue dogs like it when people show us kindness and

concern. The keeper faded once more into his bark
hiding place and I hoped his disappointment in me
would soon pass. The ancient oak tree kept its secret
well, and the time tunnel was hidden once more.
I noticed the new growth of the bluebell plants
and thought it wouldn't be long before the showy
heads would be dancing in the breeze, carpeting the
understory once more. A year turned full circle.

Nothing else for it but to pick up the pink ball and
go home, keeping my tail low.

I can't believe it's a whole year that I've been with
my people; rescue dog and now very important
messenger to Athelstan with the aid of the the forest
folk. I'm just waiting very patiently for Athelstan
to send for me again. Yulia will be tapping on the
kitchen window astride the owl. I know I will be
summoned. I'm sure I'll be back soon with more
adventures!

287

If you have enjoyed reading the first book in 'The Secret Adventures of Rolo' series you may like to join Rolo's fan club or share nature observations with him for his newsletter.

Please see the website www.debievans.com for more details and always remember to ask parental permission.

The Secret Adventures of Rolo